Saba's
Two-Year
Hiatus

Saba's ~~Two-Year~~ Hiatus

Novel by

MAURICE MASOZERA

Published by Ijenii LLC

Cover Design: Ali Sh
Editing: Jaime Brockway | Eliza Dee
Book Design and Typesetting: Enchanted Ink Publishing

ISBN: 979-8-9867668-2-9 (E-book)
ISBN: 979-8-9867668-0-5 (Paperback)
ISBN: 979-8-9867668-1-2 (Hardcover)

Library of Congress Control Number: 2022917740

To my *family* and *friends*.

To my brother Aladin and my friend Egide *gone too soon*.

CHAPTER 1

.

The First Ride

○·

Mud projectiles shot at us like machine-gun fire as I rammed the car through the muck, sending my new employee handbook flying off the dashboard into the lap of one of my clients.

Rain was pouring outside, its rhythmic crackling against the roof adding an ominous sound to the upbeat tune playing out of the car stereo, and thunder intermittently interrupted the music after every flash of lightning. Streams of water ran off curvy hill slopes and rushed down into a steep valley below with violent force. I had my high beams on and was the sole car on the dirt road going up to Ruhengeri. The rainstorm veiled the moonlight, and the darkness was thick and palpable.

I kept the gear stick of my company's Toyota RAV4 in second and third, but the car continually slipped in the mud.

I pulled my phone closer to my face again. We'd gone off-road about twenty minutes ago. Sweat dripped from my underarms down my rib cage despite the cold weather outside.

My left hand gripped the steering wheel like a tree in a windstorm as I checked Google Maps for the third time. No annotations of hazardous road conditions appeared on the app, no flash flood warnings; only a smooth light blue line connecting to a red dot that marked our destination.

"Sorry for the terrible road," I said. My guests were silent. I waited a little longer to hear another voice besides my own, but no one inside the vehicle was talking; no one moved other than to occasionally peek through the window to get a sense of where we were.

The road was a combination of mud and stones from volcanic residue. Ruhengeri is a town in the northwest of Rwanda on the Albertine Rift, an active continental drift zone stretching from Lake Albert to Lake Tanganyika in East Africa.

"Google Maps doesn't account for road conditions, I guess," I mumbled on, hoping to extract a few words from my reluctant listeners. My words fell flat again. Everyone else remained silent.

Dan, who sat next to me, reached from his seat and wiped the fogged-up windshield clean in a circular motion using the back of his hand. He noticed I was struggling to keep the fog off the windshield.

"Thanks, man!"

The gesture gave me a bit of comfort. I admired Dan for lending a hand, literally. His safety sort of depended on it. But it was nice of him. Our situation was my fault, as I should have known that the road was impassable. We could have safely waited somewhere for the rain to clear before driving on it . . .

"Oh, crap!" I yelled as the car hit a bump and stopped moving.

I rocked the steering wheel back and forth and pressed the gas pedal. The back tires spun around, spewing mud on the car frame with loud, sputtering slaps.

I stopped the car engine and looked through the windshield but couldn't see a thing. The fog reclaimed its territory on the windshield before long, and Dan was clearing his side of the window, distracted by what appeared to be a cliff edge at the right end of the muddy road. Raindrops hit the windshield so hard that it seemed as if they would drill a hole through it and shatter it at any minute.

I slowly opened the door to look outside, and a gust of wind and rain rushed inside the car and splashed my face. I shot my body back inside the car and shut the door again.

"Terrible weather," I said.

"Dude, this is insane!" Dan said. "Did you know the road would be this bad?"

"What are we going to do now?" Karen said from the back seat in a panicked voice.

"The tires could be stuck in the mud. I'll go out and check, okay?" I looked outside and slowly opened the door again but then slammed it shut.

There was a time when I wasn't afraid to walk in the rain—my elementary school days, when I used to play outside with my friends. "It's like taking a shower in the wind," we would say. I didn't care that rain would soak my khaki shorts. Instead, I would run toward the rain and frolic like a baby elephant in the mud. Times had changed.

"Dan, do you know how to drive a stick shift?"

"Yeah, I do."

"Can you take the wheel, please? Maybe rocking the vehicle will get it going again."

My hand grabbed the door handle as I braced for the rain showers to bury me outside.

When I jumped out of the car, rainwater soaked my clothes in seconds. I walked to the rear to check what was wrong, trying to lift each foot before the swampy ground could swallow it, but still my shoes sank into the mud.

Dan had jumped over the gearbox to take over the steering wheel without getting out of the car. Elise, who sat next to Karen, peeked through the window, her shadowed face in the glass. She had climbed onto the back seat to observe what was happening at the back of the car.

The road had no gutter on either side. Heavy rains had eroded the road surface over time and created a massive pothole, which had trapped the back left wheel. As I stood there, the rain became more severe and washed down my body like spray from a garden hose.

I wiped the rain off my forehead, my thoughts scrambling as I figured out what to do. The music had stopped playing. The only noises were those of splattering rain hitting against the car's roof and streaming water flowing between my feet. I checked the right tire and touched its mud-covered tread, wondering how I would push a car full of people out of a muddy pothole by myself.

The car was the only source of light on the dark road. I looked in front of the vehicle at the edge of the beaming headlights and saw a shadow of a man wearing a long raincoat, walking fast in our direction.

"Hey, hey . . . !" I yelled at the top of my voice to get his attention.

The man heard my call as he got closer to the car. Without saying a word, he approached the vehicle and examined the tires.

"Go there!" he barked at me, pointing toward the left edge of the car's rear. He leaned on the right side of the vehicle, and I grabbed the other side, gesturing to Dan to get ready to steer the car out of the hole.

"One, two, three . . . push!" We started rocking the car at the count of three.

Dan maneuvered the car to ensure it didn't veer off the road. On the third attempt, the wheels spun out of the pothole so fast that my grip slipped and sent me sprawling into the mud behind it.

"Asante sana!" I collected myself off the ground and thanked the man who had helped us. I extended my wrist instead of my mud-covered hand to show appreciation. He touched it with the tips of his fingers and hurried away in the direction he had been going.

Rainwater continued to cut across the road, creating its own paths and rushing downhill before falling off a cliff into a deep valley below.

Drenched to the skin, I hopped back inside the car on the passenger side. Contrary to our company's rules, I let Dan drive the rest of the way. At that point, I was contemplating losing my job—a job I had just started. My company, Msafiri Bora Tours (MBT), sent customer satisfaction surveys to tourists after every trip. Because it was a small team, the CEO would read every review himself. I could picture a description of a near-death experience, with tourists stranded in the rain in the middle of nowhere. Corrective measures would undoubtedly be on their way; or, in noncorporate words, they would fire me.

My failure to prepare for these hazards as a novice employee felt like a dagger to my heightened sense of responsibility. For goodness' sake, I was the tour guide here! It was my job to know where to go and how to get there safely.

Maybe taking this job had been a mistake. It hadn't even occurred to me to ask more experienced drivers at the company for tips about driving on this route. My hopes had been dim when I'd come into this new trade, and my fears were seemingly confirmed. Almost everyone I knew, friends and family, thought it was a bad idea for me to change careers to become a tour guide.

As a natural people pleaser who lives in a community where what others think of you matters more than it should, I had resisted disappointing my family and friends. Eventually, I made my own choices regardless of their approval. I was thirty-three years old; the opportunity to reinvent myself was closing.

I had failed to convince my parents that being a tour guide was an acceptable career choice. My younger brother was in medical school, and my older sister had a master's in economics. I was basically the least educated kid in my family.

My college degree in social sciences gave me a job at a nonprofit in Kigali. I held it for several years, until I grew uninspired and unhappy with office work. It was then that I became a travel agent . . .

"We made it!" Karen shouted. We had just reached a tarmac road with public lighting.

Dan drove the rest of the way, following Google Maps' directions. Rainwater was still dripping off my forehead. My clothes were swampy and covered in mud, my body was cold, and my feet were floating on iced rainwater that had permeated my sneakers, soaking my socks . . .

"What do you mean, the road is dangerous?" the lodge receptionist said. He stood behind the counter, dwarfed by a massive brown painting of long-horned royal cows locally known as Inyambo.

"We almost veered off the road into the ravine." I stared at the guy with wide eyes, surprised he didn't know the condition of the road that most of his customers took to come to his lodge.

"What road did you take?" he said. "You must have gone through the old road. I believe the old road is closed, though." He walked behind his oval-shaped desk to collect receipt papers from the printer machine.

I was at the front of the line, waiting to be checked in. Dan was next to me. He carried the weight of his lumpy backpack by a single shoulder strap. The girls were right behind us.

"Wait, there's another road?" I said.

"Yeah, a smooth paved one that goes from the city center to this lodge," the receptionist said.

"You got to be kidding me!" Dan shook his head. He was wearing a blue hat backward, with only the letter *S* written in big white font.

"I can't believe you guys came through that road. It's in terrible shape," the receptionist said.

"No," Dan said, "it's in deadly shape!"

"Here are your room keys, sir. It's down the hallway to your right," he replied in a lackluster voice. A couple of other tourists wearing rain jackets were waiting in line. Besides being the country's breadbasket, Ruhengeri is one of the most visited regions of Rwanda.

I collected my room keys after everyone in the group I was traveling with got theirs. One visitor in line looked at me with a smile, bouncing his gaze from my face to my dirt-covered jeans as if to say, "What happened to you?"

When I got to my bed, I checked the valuables in my bag to ensure they weren't wet. Our four hiking tickets to Mount Bisoke were still dry in my insulated backpack pocket. Relieved, I put the tickets in my nightstand drawer.

After taking a hot shower and cleaning up, I collapsed on the bed surface on top of tidy patchwork quilts. I allowed myself to be human again and feel the rush of emotions.

The back of my head sank between my hands as I drifted into a slumber, contemplating what had just happened on my first work assignment.

Hiking Bisoke

○·

I woke up to the sound of nightingales, a chorus of morning birds too eager to start the day, too excited to greet the first rays of sunrise. Other than the birds, the mountains were still asleep outside. They lay undisturbed next to each other, tucked underneath a thick morning fog.

As the clock needle hit 6 a.m., I stood next to the open window and took in a lungful of fresh air. My heart was full of optimism, the kind that a new day brings almost irrationally. The cheer of Mother Nature's welcome gave me hope for what was to come.

Everything was uncharted territory for me in this new job. The one-day training and employee guide I had received before embarking on my first assignment had failed to make up for my lack of real-world experience. MBT was a young and lean company. Mr. Sadiki, the company's CEO, had taken a chance on his new employees. He believed training junior staff not only was easier and cheaper than hiring more experienced professionals but also fostered stronger company loyalty. I marveled that I had gotten this job without prior experience in the tourism industry. I had taken a shot in the dark, and here I was.

My three guests and I drove to the local tourism office, tailing a Toyota Land Cruiser driven by other tourists staying at the same lodge we were. We zigzagged through rocky unpaved roads that cut through a green eucalyptus forest before reaching the park entrance, where visitors' cars had turned the muddy parking lot to mush.

"I don't think you can hike in those." After punching our admission tickets, the park ranger pointed at Elise's shoes.

"What should I do?" Elise asked, staring at her sneakers.

"You can rent hiking boots here for three dollars," the ranger replied, adjusting the weight distribution of the lime-green backpack he was carrying. The local currency is Rwandan francs, but US dollars are generally accepted, especially in places that cater to tourists.

"Don't worry about it. I'll get you hiking boots," I interjected, realizing yet another detail I had failed to account for.

Dan had his waterproof boots on. I gave a ten-dollar bill to the tour guide and got three pairs of boots for myself and the two women.

The lead park ranger was in an army-green uniform, flanked by three protection and patrol team members in military fatigues. Two of the officers had AK-47s strapped on their shoulders. The lead ranger explained they would hike with the group in case we met angry buffalos on our way up. Virunga National Park, where Mount Bisoke is located, is home to wild mammals. Here, you can find mountain gorillas, elephants, and buffalos.

As soon as we had our gear on, the lead park ranger marched in front of the group. Another ranger walked behind the queue, next to two armed guards, all three walking at the pace of the slowest person in the group.

Foreigners like Dan, Karen, and Elise made up most of MBT's customers. Although the price of admission to Virunga National Park and surrounding attractions was lower for nationals, hiking as a hobby hadn't yet caught on with locals. Rwanda is called the land of a thousand hills for a reason. Most locals walk these hills back and forth as they go about their business every day and don't feel the need to pay to do so for recreation.

Mount Bisoke, however, is no hill. At more than twelve thousand feet in altitude, it is one of the tallest mountains in the region. Bisoke is a dormant volcano in the Virunga Forest, along the chain of mountains elevated across the western branch of the East African Rift. This developing tectonic plate boundary is gradually tearing the eastern part of Africa, which sits on the Somali Plate, off the rest of the continent on the African Plate. Rift activity in this region is responsible for Mount Bisoke and some of the world's tallest mountains, including Africa's highest peak and the world's tallest free-standing mountain, Mount Kilimanjaro.

Unlike the night before, a blue sky stretched over the horizon with sharp colors. I could see cloud-capped volcanoes from a distance. Green fields lay below and clothed the majestic chain of volcanoes, towering into the sky with imposing size. The breathtaking view encouraged our tired legs to keep going up the muddy and slippery path.

We hiked Mount Bisoke for about an hour and a half. The friendly chatter from the tourists faded into the weary sounds of boots and bodies splashing in mud. I could hear my companions' whistling rhythmic breathing as we hit some steeper sections of the climb.

Rangers walked in front and carved a path through a dense and wet undergrowth—a thick sheet of lush vegetation intertwined with woody vines covered the mountain slopes. On the muddy route up the mountain, rangers cut shrubs and plants with a machete where the forest had reclaimed its territory.

I planted my climbing stick on the ground and looked behind me to check on my team. Karen was the only person in sight, but I could hear others walking nearby behind the bush. I just couldn't see them. A thick fog descended on the forest, obstructing visibility and muting the sharp green colors of the tropical forest, which looked like a scene from the movie *Jurassic Park*.

The sky was cloudy above us as we journeyed up the mountain.

"I am so tired," Karen panted.

She had made the mistake of carrying her backpack, which added weight to her body. Both girls had brought their backpacks, but Dan had Elise's on his shoulder.

"I can help carry your bag, Karen."

She handed it to me without saying a word. The park rangers led the group, followed by Dan and Elise as we climbed in an increasingly spaced-out line formation. I, Karen, and two other tourists were lagging a few meters behind.

The steep climb gave place to a small flat surface where a memorial stone fitted into the ground.

"Dian Fossey's grave!" I exclaimed.

The experience was as new to me as it was to my tourist guests. Luckily, someone else oversaw this portion of the trip. I didn't have to worry about taking a wrong turn in the forest.

"This is her grave?" Elise asked.

The nickname locals gave her, Nyiramachabelli, was inscribed on top of her gravestone, which read:

Dian Fossey, 1932–1985. No one loved gorillas more. Rest in peace, dear friend. Eternally protected in this sacred ground, for you are home where you belong.

"I have such great respect for this woman," Dan said. He rested his chin on his climbing stick, reading the memorial plaque. "She lived here alone—such a badass!"

"She wasn't alone. She was living with her friends—the gorillas!" said one ranger before he ordered us to take a break for a few minutes.

Hagenia trees surround Dian's final resting place. Born in the Bay Area, Dian Fossey was one of the most prominent animal conservationists of the twentieth century.

An adventurous spirit, she left her home country in the mid-1960s and came to live in the African jungle to research primates and fend off poachers. Local accounts of her life said she would sometimes chase poachers with a knife. She paid for it with her life a couple of decades later—but not before she had set up one of the world's longest-running research centers on primates.

Dian Fossey and her colleagues, Jane Goodall and Birute Galdikas, were the three most prominent scholars in their field. They studied the great apes in their natural habitat in the '60s and '70s. Kenyan-British archaeologist Louis Leakey, who collaborated with them, nicknamed the all-female team the "Trimates." Louis and his wife, Mary Leakey, performed research at Olduvai Gorge in Tanzania that led to discoveries that suggested East Africa was the cradle of human evolution . . .

After a fifteen-minute break, the park rangers signaled the group to resume the hike.

I breathed a happy sigh. My decision to become a tour guide felt validated for the first time. I couldn't contain my excitement about visiting the primatology and conservation history site. As we walked away, I turned around and glanced, one last time, at Dian Fossey's grave.

After three hours of hiking, the temperature dropped. A gust of darkness and chilly winds welcomed us as we neared the top of the mountain. I took my jacket out of my backpack and added an extra layer of protection to my freezing body. The exercise of climbing up the hill had kept me warm enough until now. My group and I gathered our strength and hiked the last stretch to the crater lake at the top of the mountain.

Clouds hovered over the lake on top of Mount Bisoke. Green vegetation clothed her edges, and a raised earth surface jealously guarded the waters she had collected from the sky over centuries past.

We sat down at a spot overlooking the lake. The sound of Elise's DSLR shutter interrupted the otherwise silent scenery.

The journey back down was more challenging than the way up. The muddy path squished underneath our feet and made it a point to drop everyone into the mud at least a dozen times.

o · o · o · o · o · o ·

WHEN WE GOT BACK, WE saw our lodge had lit a fire outside. People sat around the crackling firewood, bundled in blankets to isolate their bodies against the cold weather outside. They drank Primus, the local brew, and watched the flames glare, the fire lighting up their faces in bright orange color.

After taking a shower and changing their mud-covered clothes, my guests and a few others joined the group around the fireplace to drink and smoke.

I sat at the bar counter, glancing at my group resting near the fireplace like a parent watching his children. I was relieved that this day had gone well. A few mishaps notwithstanding, I thought I might have a chance to call this trip successful. If this group's reviews didn't sink my nascent career, I could only go up from here. In the end, I expected two fine reviews and one terrible one. My suspicion was that the one poor review would come from Dan, but I was counting on the other two in the group to forgive my rookie mistakes and balance things out. Losing this job was not an option, not this early.

My arms hugged the three water bottles I ordered at the bar as I walked to my guests near the fireplace.

"Here's water I brought for you; stay hydrated!" I handed the first bottle to Karen and turned to Dan and Elise.

"Thanks! Just put theirs on the ground, Saba. I don't think hydration is their problem now," Karen said.

Dan and Elise were snuggling under a blanket, kissing.

"Wait, Saba, come sit with me—I don't want to be the third wheel," Karen said as I started back toward the bar counter.

I took a blanket and sat next to Karen. Next to us, Elise and Dan kept making out; their legs were sticking out. The blankets were small, but Dan and Elise insisted on sharing one, even though the lodge had many to spare.

A glowing flame danced in front of us, its burning fire confined by a circular concrete pit.

One tourist boasted that he had only fallen twice during the descent. Everyone talked about how proud they were; they'd made it up the mountain and back. They shared their experience with excitement, recalling how big the mountain was, its forest and trees, and how massive worms hid underneath the leaves. Everyone was chatting—except Dan and Elise.

Dan was kissing her, stroking the back of her head, and exhaling puffs of cigarette smoke up her open mouth and nostrils, which she seemed to enjoy, somehow.

"Do you want to go for a walk?" Karen looked at me, squinting from the secondhand smoke.

The fire flared, and I could feel the heat brushing off my face as we walked away and headed toward the exit, then down the stairs of the side entrance gate. Karen's hand brushed mine as we walked down the stairs with caution.

Uneven volcanic rocks paved the area outside the lodge. We wandered around until we found a small ramp to sit on.

"I like that we've been on top of that volcano." Karen pointed at the shadow of Mount Bisoke, which towered over the horizon. The clear sky provided enough light from the stars to see the shadows of volcanoes at night.

"Yes! I'm happy you guys liked it. I hope the trip was a success."

"It was!" Karen looked at me, surprised it wasn't apparent.

"That's what I thought too . . . well, except for yesterday," I said. "Sorry, I let you guys down. I should have known things better as your tour guide."

"Don't worry about that; you're good," she reassured me.

"Thanks, Karen! Please remember that when you fill out the customer satisfaction survey." I smiled.

"You send a customer satisfaction survey after this?"

"Yeah, that's how the boss knows whether we're doing a good job. He'll be looking at your three reviews carefully, I'm sure," I said. "Speaking of which—you're looking at a new hire. This is my first job assignment."

"Oh, congratulations!"

"Thanks!" I said. "To be honest, I wasn't sure about this job until recently. Hope you guys choose our company for your next adventure."

"Maybe we will."

"How long are you in Rwanda?" A couple other tourists walked by us as I adjusted my sitting position.

"I'm here for about a week. I'll go home for three months after this trip but will be back," she said. "After completing my master's degree next month, I'll do a post-grad fellowship here later this summer. It's a typical path for young, aspiring professionals in my field," she said. "Dan and Elise live here, though; they moved to Kigali last year and have jobs there."

"What was your degree in?"

"I have an international relations bachelor from Emory University and a master's in the same field from Georgetown University. Enough about me, though; tell me about yourself, Saba!"

"Well, I'm starting a new career myself. This trip was just my first job assignment at MBT—it was my first ever as a tour guide. I bet you could tell, right?" I smiled. "When I took this job, everyone warned me against it."

"Why would they warn you against it?"

"Well, being a tour guide isn't a viable career path here. It's seasonal and volatile. It's what you do when you can't get a 'real' job."

The cold stones on the ramp we sat on warmed up a little from body heat. We sat next to each other, facing the same direction in a long-sitting rest.

Flickering stars bloomed in the sky above us in a cosmic show. But they struggled to present their act in its full splendor because the shadows of tall volcanic mountains obstructed them.

"Do you ever doubt your career choices?" I asked.

"All the time," Karen said. "But I knew I wanted to move abroad from an early age. During my senior year of high school, I took a trip to Senegal and fell in love with the place. It was just a matter of time before I could come back," she said. "For two years, I lived there as a volunteer, between my undergraduate and master's degrees."

"Senegal is great! I've never been, but I've always felt a connection to the country. I read many works by Senegalese authors in high school: Léopold Sédar Senghor, Cheikh Anta Diop, and others. Senegalese authors dominate much of the Francophone literature in Africa, you know."

"I do. Have you read Mariama Bâ?"

"I don't think so." I trapped my hands between my legs to warm them. I had left my mud-covered jacket in my room after returning from our trip.

"She's one of my favorite authors," Karen said. "I have one of her books, called *So Long a Letter*, if you want to borrow it."

Moving Out

o · o · o · o · o · o · o · o · o · o · o · o · o · o · o · o · o · o · o ·

M oving boxes littered the room. An old Motorola phone
charger, running shoes, and a bunch of clothes were
strewn all over the floor. I pulled back the curtains on
the small traditional window that faced the back of our shared house
but didn't turn off the sole lightbulb inside my room. The wind
knocked outside the window; it shook the loose locking handle as if
it would tear it off the frame and sling it inside my room.

I sat on the floor, sifting through my three-drawer dresser and
packing my valuables into a moving box, one item at a time. Each
represented a time of my life.

In the bottom drawer, I found a yellowed copy of my favorite
Tintin comic book, *On a marché sur la Lune, or Explorers on the
Moon*. Its musty smell filled my nose when I exhumed it from under-
neath wrinkled papers and old books. The book looked like it had

grown ears on its edges. I had kept it since I was nine; it was a gift from my cousin Seth when his family had moved to Canada.

An old photograph of five-year-old me in sapphire shorts and clenched fists. My dad had just bought me my first and only bike—a BMX knockoff. I was taking the bike for a spin when my dad took the picture.

The color photograph caught my eye for a moment before I put it in a moving box on top of my passport and college diploma. I wanted to hold on to this moment a little longer—this house, this neighborhood—but it was time, once again, for me to move.

Things had changed over the many years I had called this place home. It was the first place I'd rented after college. I'd teamed up with a college friend as soon as I got my first full-time job. We'd decided we shouldn't live at our parents' houses anymore, so we'd rented our own place.

Now my friend was about to get married to his college sweetheart. I had agreed to move somewhere else and give them the house.

I would miss the easy commute to work and the bustling open market; even the theatrics of our neighbor had somehow become part of the familiar charm. Our neighbor was a single mom of a teenage boy who had set up a dive bar in her backyard. The loud screams and euphoric giggles of binge drinkers who regularly visited the place at night didn't bother me anymore. I had learned to sleep through them as if they were a bedtime song.

The door to my room swung open—it was my friend Guido. He ducked his head underneath the door frame and walked in.

"Saba, are you ready yet?"

"Almost." I threw a pair of scissors and a drained blue ballpoint pen into a moving box. "The big items are ready to go. I just need to pack a few small things, and that should be it."

"Look at you—you're killing it at life, bro!" he said. "Getting a new apartment, and I heard you got a new job too? You should get a wife, and your life would be perfect!" He smiled.

"I like how you look at things, Guido," I replied. "You know, I feel like I'm being kicked out of my house. I have to move because my roommate is getting married and staying here. As for the recent career change, the jury is still out. And don't get me started on the wife situation."

"Don't talk like that, Saba," Guido said. "You have everything you need to succeed. I am sure you'll meet a nice girl who makes you happy."

"Well, I met this girl a couple weeks ago on my first work assignment. I could feel myself becoming more interested in her and wanted to see her again."

"You should ask her out."

"She was visiting from America for a short time, but she told me she'd be back in Rwanda around July or August."

"I've been thinking about my career as well. I want to work in finance, but I need to sort some things out first."

The boards of my disassembled bed stood against the wall next to its wooden slats and a full-size mattress. I had put all the parts in one corner, ready to pick up, except for the screws and bolts, which I kept in my pocket.

"All right, let's pack; the truck driver is here," Guido said. "He charges by the hour, so we should start loading the truck."

Guido grabbed one of the bed boards in one hand, picked up my desk chair in another, and left the room. Guido and I had attended the same high school, Lycée Notre–Dame de Cîteaux, and had remained friends since. He had arranged for a guy to help me move and transport my bed and furniture. For things to get done around here, you have to know a guy.

By the time we finished loading the truck, the skies above us had turned gray. The wind blew a few clouds off the heavens, but many floated just above the ground's surface, wrapping the dark green hill slopes below in a grayish tint.

"I don't have tie-down straps," the truck driver said, "so one of you will have to ride in the back and keep the furniture from falling."

He arranged the last piece of the cargo in his truck bed. The truck was a blue Daihatsu Delta that looked in good condition, except for the side mirrors: they were bigger than usual. The artisanal welding job on the mirror frames was already showing corrosion.

"Don't worry about it, boss. I'll ride in the back," I said. "Guido, you can take the front seat if you prefer." I hopped in the back of the truck, and the driver went back inside the car.

Everyone was in the truck now, except for Guido. He stood by undecided, his six-foot-eight body frame imposing.

"Do you think it's going to rain?" Guido looked at me. His head still towered over me, even as I was sitting on the truck bed's side rail.

"It sure looks like it, doesn't it?"

"I mean, before we get to the house," he said.

"It's a twenty-minute drive, so I think we can beat the rain to the house."

"Are you sure?"

"Dude, what's the matter?" I said. "Let's go!"

He climbed into the back, swinging his giant limbs over the truck's tailgate. Guido, a giant of a man, had been on our high school basketball team. His size and stern demeanor had always struck fear in the hearts of our rivals from other schools.

About fifteen minutes after we left the house, it started raining. First came light showers for about one minute, and then heavy rain poured down. We had packed the furniture inside the truck bed. A plastic bag covered the mattress on top of the wood slats.

The wind whipped against my shivering body, and rain hit my face like water from a showerhead. With nowhere to hide, I firmly grabbed the side rail and braced for the showers to drench my body.

Rain swooshed and swooshed again in a rhythmic tide. Cars on the road passed us with their high beams on and hazards flashing; their tires pushed against a bulging trail of rainwater that had flooded the road.

We drove past dark grayish-green trees planted along the road in a straight line. Only the trees looked happy to receive the rain. They danced and rocked back and forth as rain droplets hit their leaves, dripping off and soaking the ground that nurtured them.

"Guido, are you okay?"

"You said it wouldn't rain," he shouted over the whirring rain.

"What? Sorry about that; we're almost there now."

Guido's face looked pale. His left hand clung to the metal bar mounted on the truck bed's headboard. He wiped raindrops off his face with such violence that I thought he would peel off his skin. He seemed mad at heaven itself for allowing gray skies to storm his life.

The rain kept pouring down until the truck drove through the gates of my new house. As soon as we arrived, Guido jumped off the truck bed and took shelter inside.

I followed him. "Bro, is everything okay?"

"I need a moment," he said. "Don't wait for me to unload the truck. I'll go dry off."

I opened the front doors wide to allow easier access into the house as we unpacked the truck. In the meantime, Guido went and locked himself in the bathroom.

I paid the driver in cash when he and I finished carrying the furniture off the truck, much of which we had just dropped in the living room in haste. I went back inside to check on Guido; he was lying on the bed in the guest room. My new roommate, Kamana, was a friend of Guido's. In fact, Guido had introduced us after hearing that I was looking for a roommate to sublet a house with.

I changed into a new T-shirt and went into the kitchen to make black tea. Rain was still pattering against the roof.

Vapor rose from the kettle as it boiled water with a whistling sound.

When I returned to the guest bedroom, Guido held his head in his hands, hunched over.

"Here." I handed him a cup of tea. "Be careful; it's hot." I sat across from him. His head emerged from the towel he had wrapped around it.

"Look, I'm sorry! I didn't know it was going to rain. I should have insisted you sit inside the car so you wouldn't get rained on," I said.

My apology was more confused than heartfelt, and it showed in the tone of my voice.

"In all the years you've known me, have you ever seen me walk or play in the rain?" Guido said.

I paused and tried to remember.

"You haven't!" he interrupted before I could respond.

I would have bet I'd seen him walk in the rain at least one day, but who keeps track of such things anyway? I had never paid attention to that detail.

"Why do you hate walking in the rain?"

He blew over his cup of tea, took a sip, and paused.

"It's a trigger," he said. "You know I saw my parents and sister getting killed during the genocide against the Tutsi, right?"

"You told me about it, yes."

"Ahem. There were heavy rains that day, too, as is usually the case in April. I was ten then, and I remember spending the night in the forest, hiding from the killers who had just murdered my family. Rain takes me back to that dark moment of my life. Showers flowed down my face and obstructed my vision as I tried to escape and watch out for the killers. The bitter smell of wet earth filled my mouth, the damp moss and wet trees, drenched clothes stuck on my shivering body—it all takes me back to that night, to the loneliness and the dread of imminent and cruel death. I remember I slept outside and stayed hidden in the bush that night. I waited for my mom to wake me up, tuck me into bed again, and tell me that the whole thing was just a bad dream, a nightmare. But that nightmare wouldn't let me wake up from it, no matter how badly I wanted things to go back to normal, to have my family back again. My family was gone: my mom, my dad, my sister, they were all gone. For good . . ."

His throat seemed to tighten, barely sounding the last few words as he recounted the gruesome ordeal he had gone through as a child. He clenched his empty cup as he struggled to stop his grief from pouring out in a stream of tears.

"That is tragic, Guido." My face fought back the tears welling in my eyes. "I can't even imagine what you went through."

"Even a professional couldn't help. Things kept coming back," he said. "The trauma has lingered for a while. If you remember, I had a painful episode in the last year of high school and have had other awful ones after that."

"I knew you were sick for a long while, and I remember you stopped coming to school and basketball practice. I always wondered what happened."

"Yeah, most people didn't know. Well, I thought the triggers would stop as I grew older, and there was no need to alarm everyone, but it hasn't worked so far."

24

"Man, that's some heavy stuff you're dealing with," I said. "You're the bravest man I know, bro!"

"Don't worry about it. It might kill me one day, but until then, I've learned to live with it. I just need a moment, and I'll be fine," he said. "Can I get another tea?"

The Mille Collines

○·○·○·○·○·○·○·○·○·○·○·○·○·○·○·○·○·○·○·

We walked into a poolside bar to the sound of a saxophone and chatter from a bar crowd. People sat toward the west end of the pool near a small stage tucked in a corner underneath the shadow of bamboo trees. The lead singer jerked his arms and legs at the rhythm of the music without crumpling his clothes, a black tuxedo and a bow tie.

People occupied the tables near the stage, drowning themselves in an endless supply of alcohol and food and hoping to ease the stress of a hard workweek. A few other musicians stood next to the jazz band, their guitars still boxed, and anxiously waited for their turn to entertain the crowd. The floor lights illuminated the trees planted all around the place in rainbow colors, creating the impression of a party in a small, decorated jungle. Animated lights wrapped around the green vegetation in the hotel's backyard.

It was a Thursday night, and Hôtel des Mille Collines was hosting a soundcheck party for Kigali's flagship music festival, KigaliUp.

Karen and I walked around with our phones in hand and took a few pictures of the view. The words *Hôtel des Mille Collines* flashed through the clear water, permanently written on the swimming pool floor, as they are in the history books.

We weaved through the crowd for a while before finding empty seats next to the pool at the edge of the thatched bar roof that had just been vacated by two other customers on an early night out.

"My neck is sore. I'm still jet-lagged from my flight last weekend." Karen grimaced, holding the back of her neck as I took a seat next to her.

"Drink some wine; it will help." I flipped through the drink menu on the table.

"Wine will help?" she said without taking her eyes off her phone screen. The bright light from her phone cast a glow on her face.

I sat facing Karen and the backdrop of Kigali's rolling hills. The flickering city lights revealed the curves of the city's topography at night.

The weather had allowed Karen to wear a sleeveless blue satin dress that night. I was wearing a striped white shirt tucked into a pair of khaki jeans.

"So, what have I missed in the few months I was gone?" she said. "Are you still enjoying your job as a tour guide?"

"I got better at it since the last time we met, I promise." I smiled.

The couple who sat at our table before we arrived had left a leaflet behind. The flyer's cover page featured a picture of artist Ismaël Lô holding a guitar in his bright yellow boubou, a traditional West African robe.

"Did you know Ismaël Lô will play for the first time in this year's festival? Tonight is the soundcheck party for KigaliUp; that's why we have so many people at the hotel." I read through the KigaliUp brochure that event organizers conveniently put on tables around the bar to promote the event.

"I missed his performance when living in Senegal during my Peace Corps years. It's great I finally get to see him perform."

"How can you miss Ismaël Lô's performance?" I shrugged.

"Hey, I was living in the middle of nowhere, in the Kédougou Region. I like Ismaël and all, but I wasn't up for the ten-hour commute to Dakar, where he was performing," she explained.

"Fair enough!" I said. "What was it like living in rural Senegal?"

"There wasn't much going on, really! My house was near the main road in my village, and I could hear people going to the market in the morning on their donkey carts. The weather is scorching hot, and because of that, no one works past noon."

"So, what did you do in the afternoons?"

"We just sat around in the shade of a giant baobab every day, drinking ataya tea and constantly having the same conversation: It's hot today, isn't it? Yes, it's hot." She smiled.

"You know, I'm five years older than you, but it sounds like you have more street cred than me!" I said. "I have a lot of respect for people who live and work in rural communities where they need the most help. You must be a pro at bucket showers by now, huh?"

"I've had a lot of bucket showers, yes."

"The trick is to scoop the water sparingly, or you risk running out before rinsing off," I said.

"I used a plastic cup."

When a server came to our table, I ordered African tea, filet mignon brochettes with vegetables, and green banana fries. Karen ordered a glass of wine to go with the food.

A young crowd near the small stage broke into loud cheers as a local band, known for its poetic love songs, took to the stage. They sang a fan-favorite song called "Uri Mwiza," which means "you're beautiful." The band was one of the few old-school groups that bridged the generational divide in music taste.

"Do you know where you'll go after your fellowship ends?" I asked, turning my attention back to Karen.

"I want to stay in the region, preferably a French-speaking country," she said. "My guess is that my organization will send me back to West Africa, given my previous experience in Senegal."

"Burundi or the Congo are options if you want to stay in the region in a French-speaking country."

"I've been applying to jobs in different countries, but Burundi would be nice," she said. "I'll take the first job that comes my way, to be honest. Given I have student loans to pay and limited experience, I can't be too picky." She sipped from her glass of pinot noir to drown her anxieties with alcohol.

The wind brushed against my face. It was nice outside. They had built the hotel on the upper side of a hill, providing a charming view of the expansive city.

"I think you would be a terrific employee wherever you end up, Karen!" I said. "I mean, I'd hire you."

"Ha! Do you have a job to offer?"

"I would if I did."

"Seriously, I should know my next job by now," she said. "Too much uncertainty!" She tilted her head backward to empty her wineglass.

I watched Karen as she sat on the bamboo chair across from our table, her shoulders pulled back. The playing band distracted her eyes. We could clearly hear them but could barely see them because of the crowd that congregated around the musicians.

"You don't have to wait for a job to visit Burundi. I could take you for a visit so you can get a feel for the country."

"Yeah?!" Karen turned her face from the playing band and looked at me. Her silent look sent my heartbeat racing. My head resisted the urge to take back the offer of a getaway trip together for a few seconds so I could hear what she had to say. I waited a few more seconds for an answer until the silence became unbearable.

"It would be fun, I think," I broke. "Besides, it would give me a reason to go back as well."

"When were you last in Burundi?" she asked, lowering her eyes back to her phone on the table.

"I haven't been since my parents moved to Rwanda after the war. It also didn't help that they were having a civil war of their own for a while."

I had been thinking about my childhood neighborhood, and the day I would get a chance to visit again after such a long time. I wondered if the place looked the same as when my family and I had left and was looking forward to finding out.

The Office Dilemma

As you can see, we need to investigate alternative routes! All these companies saturate the market," Mr. Sadiki, the company's CEO, yelled from across the conference room, interrupting his deputy's presentation.

Mr. Sadiki stood in the back of the conference room behind everyone else during the presentation. His six-foot-four frame paced back and forth. During his deputy's presentation, he yelled his thoughts across, making it a point to interrupt and challenge him. He scanned his employees in the room with his massive eyeballs that peeked over low-hanging glasses, like a lord watching over his fiefdom. Monday meetings were customary, and all fourteen employees were required to attend, unless they were on a tour.

"Hey, do you know why my name isn't on the board?" I whispered to a colleague next to me.

"No!" he said. "You should ask the boss." He pointed at the

deputy CEO, who oversaw the company's operations and was, incidentally, Mr. Sadiki's cousin.

A company-wide schedule for all trips hung on a whiteboard opposite the office entrance on the ground floor. That was where the trip planner matched the names of tour guides with their respective destinations every week using a dry-erase marker.

When my name had first appeared on this board, it had been thrilling. My name had been next to a token reservation number, with "Mount Bisoke" written in the destination column. I hadn't felt that responsible since maybe the time my high school basketball coach had called me from the bench during a close elimination game against our rival school.

However, when I'd walked into my office this morning, my name didn't have a destination as it usually did every week. It had been erased from the rotation. Mr. Sadiki's cousin worked on trip planning over the weekend. Everyone found out their weekly schedules and assigned work on Monday mornings. This was about my fourth month at this company, but there were a lot of new things I was still learning, about both this trade and this organization.

"At a minimum, we should cover all destinations offered by the local airline carrier and expand our vacation bundles," Mr. Sadiki's deputy said, concluding his session. Everyone sat silently and looked at each other when the presenter opened the Q&A.

We could barely fill the small conference room and were already struggling to keep up with the local demand. Still, Sadiki's vision for the company was big. He had required everyone, including our office janitor, to be part of these weekly meetings. Was this a strategic move to ensure everyone bought into the company's grand vision?

MBT's office was a two-story building. The reception was on the left-hand side of the entrance, next to four floating desks shared among drivers in the office.

The ground floor also had a shared kitchen. The top floor housed a few additional offices, including that of the CEO, and a thirty-person-capacity conference room where we held our all-staff meetings.

"I heard RwandAir is now flying to Zambia. Maybe we should start there," Albert Baho, another employee and colleague, commented, breaking the silence after the presentation.

"Great point, AB!" Mr. Sadiki said.

"Saba, I took you out of the rotation this week, if you haven't noticed!" Mr. Sadiki said.

"Yes, I noticed," I replied quickly.

"Good! So, I want you to help our business development efforts and check for potential regional partners and tourist destinations, starting with Zambia. Try to develop a package proposal with premium and regular options," he said. "You can work with Albert on this."

"I can help, too, if you need support, Saba," the deputy CEO said after unplugging the projector from his laptop.

When I returned to my desk, I searched for RwandAir destinations on Google. Confused, I wondered why he'd taken me out of rotation and not someone else and whether this would be a permanent move. I was in the dark about my changing positions, if I still had a position in this company at all. Was this something they had planned all along?

I ran my eyes over the search results, my coffee mug in hand. Bujumbura, Lusaka, Lagos, Johannesburg . . .

MBT was a relatively new company and smaller than other, more established local players. This explained, in part, the CEO's attitude and impatience for growing our operations speedily, then.

I looked at my computer screen and navigated through a few tabs I had opened using shortcut keys.

"Here I am, doing office work again," I sighed.

After a few months on the job, I was feeling more comfortable as a tour guide, but my boss had other plans for me.

I didn't raise this with Mr. Sadiki, however. I didn't ask why they'd reassigned my job. My first experience of driving tourists around had come with challenges. However, I had since improved and led several successful trips. Even on that first trip, Karen assured me that her friends were gracious in their post-trip reviews. They didn't mention that I had driven them astray on our way to Ruhengeri. Instead, they had heaped praise on me for being a great tour guide and for giving them a memorable experience.

My phone vibrated and slid over my office desk. My heartbeat increased when I saw who had texted me.

How's your day going?

Karen! My left hand instinctively joined with my right hand at the keypad. I started typing.

The day is cool—, I wrote. Then I erased it. *It's going okay. How about yours?*

"Saba!" a loud voice yelled.

My head abruptly snapped up.

"Just to follow up on this morning's meeting, I want you to do a detailed screen of potential partners around RwandAir destinations," Mr. Sadiki said, standing in my office.

I stared at him.

"Do you get that?" he said, a bit bewildered.

"Yes, sir! I'm on it!"

This time, Mr. Sadiki wore rubber-soled shoes, which were quiet on the floor. Usually, you could almost always hear his steps and the rhythmic sound of his regular-heeled shoes approaching your office.

"I think you should also put together a budget," he continued. "I really think that we could use your project management skills, Saba," he said. "But we will see if it's the best fit for you."

"I enjoy being a tour guide, sir, and not sitting in an office all day," I said. "That's part of why I took this job."

"You will not be sitting in an office all day," he said. "You will travel to meet potential host partners once we've narrowed down the list, okay?"

"Okay, sounds good."

I glanced back at my phone as soon as my boss left my office. Karen hadn't replied to my message. After fifteen minutes, I reached out for my phone again and started typing.

Hey, I really enjoyed hanging out with you the other night. I thought we should visit the history museum or go hiking or something when you're free!

My index finger shook a little as I hit the Send button. I pushed my phone toward the other end of my office desk and held my face.

I rubbed my eyes to clear my vision and get back to work. The glare of sunlight blurred my computer screen.

The time on my phone was 12:31 p.m., and I was having difficulty focusing. I stood up and pulled the office curtains together with force. Not that they were heavy, but sunbeams traveled through the gap between the curtains, and the small stationary fan did little to keep me cool on hot days.

Mount Kigali

T he morning sun highlighted the colors of green vegetation and blooming flowers, a portrayal of overwhelming beauty. A panorama of hills drew an unending pattern over the horizon in a combination of solid edges and fading lines. A small brush of stratus scratched the sky, and cumulus floated in the heavens. It was like the work of a painter who wants to show off.

Rust-colored tiles adorned a few houses scattered in the valley. We could see the serpentine Nyabarongo River in the valley below, ushering her muddy waters between a green landscape of river grass. Despite dirt-colored waters between her banks, Nyabarongo carries with her the source of the White Nile. Her tributaries in the Nyungwe Forest are the furthest streams of the river, and they've fed a large part of human civilization for millennia past.

Mount Kigali stands 1,850 meters high. You can see it from

almost anywhere in the city that bears its name. As they do across the rest of the country's topography, hills make up most of Kigali's land surfaces. Nearly the entire country lies above a thousand meters in altitude.

The owner of the equestrian center had put a white fence around the property atop the mountain and filled it with sand that had turned grayish from recent sprinklers' watering. Karen sat tall on the back of the bay horse we had rented for a ride. She was more prepared for the hike than I was. She wore a red T-shirt and khaki hiking pants. Her Nike shoes had red foxing, matching her T-shirt and keeping her active attire discreetly stylish.

In an instant, a switch flipped in my heart. I was breathless and my knees felt paralyzed. I tried to hide it, to disguise the storm of emotions rushing through my body, but I couldn't. My beaming eyes and my smiling face betrayed me. Besides, Karen could read me like an open book.

She glanced back at me with a silent look under the cap of her riding helmet. I felt her gaze on my body as she undressed me with her eyes and scanned every page of my story, every inch of my swelling desire for her.

"Saba!"

"What, Karen?"

"It's your turn now!" She sidled around, smiling as if she meant to say something else.

I scratched my head and stood up.

Before that day, I had never ridden a horse in my life. Karen had mentioned that she liked it, so here we were. The shame of not trying at all was worse than the inevitable embarrassment.

I fitted my helmet, mounted the saddle, and started riding. I brushed the horse with my foot so as not to rattle it. It walked, trotted, cantered, and then took off with speed.

The repeated blows to my groin forced me to stand up with my knees half-bent for relief as I struggled to keep in sync with the horse's galloping cadence. I took three rounds of the compound before calling it off and dismounting from the animal's back. I limped back to Karen and collapsed on the grass next to her. She was laughing at me the entire time.

Around noon, we came down from Mount Kigali and went to one of my favorite restaurants. We pulled over on the side of a narrow street in the Nyamirambo neighborhood. I signaled to young kids, who were hanging around, to watch the car's side mirrors for a few francs until my return.

Home to both the most famous rappers and the biggest mosque in the country, Nyamirambo is the hippest neighborhood in Kigali. It's the neighborhood that never sleeps in a relatively dull city, and it's known for its cheap, flavorful food, the most popular of which bear the names of expensive cars and jewelry. Here, you will find the best Rolex in town—an omelet and veggie wrap—and Aka Benz, or "little Benz," which is pork barbecue!

"How do you like the food?" I asked Karen as she sank her teeth into her first mukeke and ugali, a dish of sleek lates, which is a fish, and cassava mush that's popular in the region.

"I love it," she said, her voice barely coming out of her full mouth.

A pleasant breeze blew through the tile-roofed balcony outside, where the restaurant had accommodated its many customers.

"Eating ugali is like taking a sleeping pill," I said.

"Yeah! I am feeling a little sleepy."

"What are your plans for the rest of the day?"

I realized how much I enjoyed spending time with Karen. Despite spending almost half a day with her, I was planning our next activity.

Dan had told me about a dance show organized by visiting students from a performing arts school in Lyon, France. The show took place later that night at a famous bar in town called Papyrus. I resented the idea of meeting Dan accompanied by Karen, however. I knew he was going to give me a hard time about it.

Dan had an interesting theory about male-female relationships. He didn't believe that a man and a woman could just be friends. He argued that, given enough time, at least one of the two had to fall for the other.

o · o · o · o · o · o ·

THE NIGHT HAD LONG FALLEN upon the hills of Kigali when our car rumbled over the cobblestone road in the Kimihurura neighborhood toward Papyrus. The sporadic yellow lights on the roadside struggled to provide clear visibility on the road ahead. Still, they somehow reflected on Karen's lip gloss.

The show had already begun when we arrived. People stood in a semicircle around performing dancers. I held Karen's hand and pulled her through the crowd toward an elevated platform to better view the show. We climbed onto the small ramp and boosted our average heights, me standing at five feet ten and Karen five feet four. Beyond the bubbling crowd, a major highway that goes up the city center lit up the horizon with the distinct yellow dotted lights of cars climbing up and disappearing behind the hills.

We peered over the enthusiastic crowd and watched the routine.

Dancers ran in circles and swung massive robes around in what appeared to be a rendition of a West African ritual dance performed by a couple of European guys. They turned their hands in the air with energy at the pitched rhythm of the djembe, at the strokes of the balafon's wooden planks.

"So, is this the contemporary dance you wanted me to see?" Karen said, unimpressed.

"It's art. Maybe we're not artistic enough to appreciate it."

I looked around to see if I could spot Dan and Elise somewhere in the crowd, but they were nowhere to be seen.

"I'm happy to hang somewhere else," Karen said. "There's a cool bar about a ten-minute drive from here, if you want to move there after this."

Thirty minutes into the event, we concluded that the show wasn't getting any better. We hopped back into the car and drove to the other bar. I had borrowed my new roommate's cherry-red Toyota Avensis for the day.

"A cold Mutzig, please," Karen said to the server when we got to Kigali Heights, a bar overlooking Kigali's convention center.

Bars serve drinks warm and cold, hence the need to specify the beverage temperature you want. Even water and soda are available in their warm variant.

"Just tonic water for me."

"What? You're not drinking?" Karen asked, annoyed.

"I'm driving, remember?" That night, I stuck to an alcohol-free diet.

"You don't have to be legalistic about it. One or two beers should be fine." She shrugged.

The Dome lit the sky in national colors: light blue, yellow, and green. Also known as the Kigali Convention Center, the Dome is the capital's flagship building. It's an oval-shaped building modeled after the traditional Rwandan house and is symbolic of modern Rwanda, which draws from her rich cultural heritage to design civil engineering projects and current public policy.

We sat on a two-seater couch on the balcony. The night was calm, and only a handful of other people sat across from us.

"Did you have a good day?" I asked, gently touching Karen's back to get her attention.

Her perfect posture left a gap between her back and the cushion. Karen pensively sat there; she let the moment sink in, absorbed in her thoughts.

"I had fun!" She paused for a while, gazing at me, then looked back in front of her and drank from her beer bottle.

Her voice sounded emotional, and her eyes were glowing from the night lamp's reflection. My heart was racing. It pulsed in my chest and pounded fast as if I had received an adrenaline shot straight into my carotid artery.

I placed my right arm on top of her couch cushion. Karen looked at me and then leaned back on the couch. She let her shoulders rest on my extended arm. I sat facing her left side as she sipped from a Mutzig bottle. I leaned in and kissed her on the cheek once. She sat still as if she was expecting it.

I waited a few seconds, then leaned in for a second time. In a timed reaction, Karen turned and met my lips halfway.

Naaj's Barbershop

A slight breeze flowed through the open door, ushering cool temperatures inside. The mood was somber in the room, and even the usual barbershop chatter had stopped. Only the sound of the clippers interrupted the silence. They vibrated, buzzed, and hummed in a continuous and echoing noise. A worn poster that hung on the wall featured an infinite variety of hairstyles, even though everyone in town wears the same haircut. Most men shave their heads bald. Wearing long hair as a man is unpopular on this side of the world and associated with irresponsible behavior; hence, the less hair you wear as a man, the better. Only artists and celebrities are exceptions to this rule.

The smell of alcohol filled the room with an antiseptic odor. Patches of hair lingered on the ground. The barber took breaks between customers for a shallow floor sweep—just enough not to gross out the next clients and make them storm out screaming in disgust.

Naaj had been running his barbershop for years, but the walls inside looked like they hadn't seen a fresh coat of paint since he moved in. It wasn't just the cracks in the wall or the white paint peeling off; everything in Naaj's shop looked like it was from a different time. Even his wall art was dated: an old poster of Maradona lifting the trophy at the 1986 World Cup in Mexico hung prominently in the room. Naaj didn't seem to care that it was 2017, that the world had new champions now or new ways of doing business.

"Saba, you're up!" Naaj said.

He pocketed two thousand Rwandan francs in cash—about three US dollars—from the other customer he had just finished shaving. The middle-aged man checked his bald head and beard trim in the mirror before adjusting his business suit and exiting the shop.

Naaj wrapped a blue drape over my body and tied it around my neck to protect my shirt from loose hair. He took a broom and cleared the floor a bit, as was his ritual. A few holes had torn through the plastic floor mat, which trapped some hair particles around its edges despite Naaj's inadequate efforts to tidy up the place.

My advice to Naaj to renovate his shop and keep up with changing times had fallen on deaf ears. This shop, just like Naaj himself, had not changed in a long time. He wore the same crumpled white T-shirt and low-hanging jeans. His jeans hung below his waistline, not as a fashion preference, but because he was too skinny.

Naaj's barbershop was a one-man show. He had no receptionist, no fancy equipment, and no complimentary massage services like the other shops in town. He didn't even have a sign at the front door that read Naaj's Barbershop or something. It was just him and his clippers.

I was one of his loyal customers who had resisted the urge to take their money elsewhere. Naaj was a childhood friend. In fact, we went to the same elementary school and sat next to each other in fifth grade in Bujumbura, Burundi, where we grew up. He was two years older than me, but we were in the same class because he had repeated a grade.

At the end of the war in 1994, Rwandans who had sought refuge in neighboring countries returned home and brought their children with them. Naaj's family settled back in Kigali in 1995, roughly the same year as mine. When we got to Kigali, my parents enrolled my siblings and me in a local private school, and we continued through high school. Naaj never went back to school. After we left Bujumbura, I didn't see him again until he opened a barbershop in my neighborhood. He had fathered a child and was working to provide for his child and wife. I was eighteen at the time and had just finished high school. Since then, I've been getting my hair cut at Naaj's barbershop.

"Wait! Today is different," I interrupted Naaj, who was getting ready to run his clippers through my hair without asking how I wanted to style it.

"What?" he said. "What do you mean?"

He turned his attention to his electric shaver machine for a moment to check the blade. It was making a broken sound. He sprayed alcohol and applied oil on the clippers from an old drip bottle, and the trick worked when he turned the machine on again.

"I want to wear long hair now," I said. "Just even it out and remove the stache, like that style on the top right of the catalog." His old wall poster had a similar hairstyle to what I wanted.

"Ha, okay! You've never picked a hairstyle like that before."

"Something different would be nice for a change."

"Okay, we'll do long hair today," he said. "For real, you've never changed hairstyles since I've known you. What happened?"

"Well, that's not true. Do you remember the hair I was wearing right when I finished high school? I used to do a Tyson—a low-cut skin fade with a head-crossing line." I referred to the hairstyle famously worn by the former heavyweight boxing champion.

"That was a long time ago!"

"Okay, I will admit! It's because of a girl," I said. "She doesn't like when I shave my head bald or wear a mustache, so there you go."

"So, you're changing your looks for her, huh?" he said. "She must be special."

"What can I say? She is!" I said. "Speaking of which, I want to take her to Bujumbura for a weekend; what should we do? She's never been before."

"Take her to the lake," he said. "You should visit our old neighborhood, too, if you get a chance," Naaj said, tilting my head back to rest on the head support fitted on the chair.

The buzzing sound of the razor became louder in my ears. The electric shaver felt hot as it slid across the surface of my skin, shaving my mustache clean off.

"I haven't been back to Bujumbura in several years, so I don't know if any of the old places are still there," I said. "Besides, we were kids back then."

"Remember our childhood friend called Babu? He used to organize football games against kids from other neighborhoods for money."

"Babuuu!" I laughed and shook my head, excited. Naaj took the electric clipper away for a few seconds as I jerked my head around.

"Babu was crazy," he said, resuming his work.

"Let me tell you, the first time I stole money from my parents was to pay him to be on his team and play against kids from the Kamenge neighborhood in the northern quarter."

"You stole money from your parents to go to that game?" He laughed.

"They would never have allowed me to play in a football tournament organized by a random kid without adult supervision."

"Well, there was always an adult at the games, remember?"

"Ya right!" I said. "You mean the homeless guy Babu paid to referee the games and break up the occasional fights? I'm sure that would have put their concerns at ease."

Naaj took a hand mirror and raised it near the back of my head to show me his work. I turned my head from different sides to check my new haircut in the mirror's reflection and nodded in approval.

"That game with Kamenge neighborhood, man. I think we lost like eight to one!"

"Those kids were super athletic!" Naaj said.

"No, those were not kids. I think they cheated and brought grown-up men to play for them . . ."

Naaj removed the drape off my shoulder and shook it behind me. I stood up from the chair and reached for three thousand francs from my wallet.

"You should reach out to Babu when you go to Bujumbura, Sab," Naaj said. "He will be happy to hear from you again after all these years. I will give you his number."

"Thanks, Naaj. It's always a pleasure to catch up," I said. "Say hello to your wife and kids for me."

CHAPTER 2

Hopeful People

o·o·o·o·o·o·o·o·o·o·o·o·o·o·o·o·o·o·o·

O ur bus drove south toward Bujumbura in Burundi. Unfazed by the bumpy road, Karen rested her head against
the window with her eyes shut. The bus sped through the
Kibira, a montane forest stretching from Rwanda to Burundi atop
the mountains of the Congo-Nile Divide.

Unable to sleep in anything moving, I pointed my gaze out the
window the entire time to observe the running world beyond our
bus.

Tiny houses made of mud bricks lined the sole asphalt road—a
likely source of economic activity. Woven baskets on their heads and
babies on their backs, women carried fresh produce to what looked
like an ambulant farmers' market. A faded red, white, and green flag
hung still on a wooden pole next to one building, as if it were glued
to it.

Buried underneath bundles of bananas twice their height,

frantic bicycle riders rushed downhill past our bus at about sixty-five kilometers an hour.

Kids tried to race our bus too. One of them wore a dirt-covered T-shirt with the word *Niyongabo* printed on his back. They stepped on an imaginary line as they saw our bus approaching. They waited for the imagined starting gun to fire before they exploded and raced our bus, laughing. Their dreams followed in the footsteps of their idol athlete—Olympic-medal-winning runner Vénuste Niyongabo—unencumbered by road hazards or the limited prospects of growing up in a rural village in one of the least developed nations in the world.

Niyongabo is a national hero. Through his athletic abilities, he worked himself up from rural Burundi to the global stage. He stole the show in Atlanta, Georgia, when he won gold in the 5,000-meter run at the 1996 Summer Olympics. He became the first person from Burundi to win an Olympic medal and raise the saltire-crossed flag on the highest Olympic podium.

The bus trip from Kigali to Bujumbura is about seven hours. We had spent about thirty minutes at the border and were to arrive on time. I adjusted my seat position, folded my arms across my chest, and closed my eyes to try and rest despite the loud ramblings of a passenger next to me.

"They took away all my plastic bags, and I had to carry everything in my hands," he vented. He had traveled to Uvira in the Congo from Kampala through Kigali City—a typical itinerary for small business operators.

"You live in Kigali, right?" he sneered to the only passenger willing to listen to him complain. "Do you think it looks like New York now? Do you think banning all the plastic bags in the country will turn your city into New York City?"

Pushing toward a greener environment, Rwanda banned plastic bags, and unsuspecting visitors are forced to carry their stuff in their hands if they don't heed the rule.

I squeezed my eyes shut tighter but couldn't help hearing everything he was saying. His short-term inconvenience clouded his ability to see the incremental progress toward a better future. Those who had lived in Kigali for a while knew how much the city had changed.

Kigali hasn't always been one of the cleanest and safest cities in Africa, as it is now known. The Rwandan capital was already in terrible shape after the civil war ended in late 1994. Roads had no sidewalks, and filth was littered everywhere. It wasn't uncommon to find human excrement next to even the most luxurious hotels. People lived in the city center as you would on an unruly camping trip. In the early 2000s, government officials set up new policies that changed the city's landscape and the culture of Kigalians in a process that seemed like an experiment in broken windows theory, or the idea that visible signs of disorder invite criminal activity and should be addressed. The city cut trees growing out of place and planted new ones all along the main avenues; it built new streets with pristine road markings and added paved sidewalks to every major street. It fined vandals and brought in an army of community police to patrol the streets.

A few years later, the men and women in purple uniforms, who ensured the city streets were orderly, disappeared. Still, people living in the city behaved as if they had never left. Over time, incivility and crime were dramatically reduced in Kigali. More and more policies came to pass, including banning plastic bags in the country and establishing a monthly public community service to clean up the streets, locally known as Umuganda.

When we arrived in Bujumbura, I felt it in my body. The humid air and comforting moisture embraced me and made my naturally dry skin whole again. We drove through the Kamenge neighborhood and then through my old community of Ngagara. Memories of our old house came flashing back. I recalled it was conveniently near a milk-processing plant called Nadel. Our house had a lovely porch, which we used to host movie nights. Because my family was one of the few with a color TV and a VHS video player, the kids in our neighborhood were good to us. We held the power of picking who got to join movie nights.

"Passports, passports, please!" a police officer yelled as soon as our bus swerved into the bustling central bus terminal next to a line of Volcano Tours buses.

I tapped Karen's arm to wake her up. Her head had collapsed on my bony shoulder during our ride as she slept throughout the trip. I reached down into my backpack's pocket for my passport and collected Karen's before placing both travel documents in the outstretched hand of the police officer, who was then inside our bus. The passenger beside me had blocked part of the walkway with his luggage.

The officer, who wore a faded blue uniform and beret, disappeared with our passports in hand.

We jumped out of the bus with backpacks on our shoulders and met the chaos outside, then paced after the police officer, zigzagging through a line of gurgling buses. There was a hubbub of travelers carrying large luggage bags. Frantic bus conductors sweltering under the heat were yelling different destinations so loud that every vein in their head strained beneath their skin.

We finally found the man seated behind a wooden desk in a quiet, dim police station. He scribbled our biographical information in columns he had traced in his wrinkled notebook to document travelers entering the country.

"Voilà!" he said in French. "Bienvenu à Bujumbura." He handed over our passports with a smile and welcomed us to the city.

Mutoka

o·o·o·o·o·o·o·o·o·o·o·o·o·o·o·o·o·o·o·

Bro, biko aye? Are you guys here?" The voice on my phone gave the casual local greeting.

"Yeah, we just got here," I said. I had just checked in to my room.

My old friend Babu planned our first dinner in town. Babu had offered to take us to a restaurant as soon as we arrived in the city. I didn't know where we would go or what kind of food we would eat. Despite my repeated pleas, Babu had refused to tell me where he had booked a table or if it was even a place that had a number you could call to book anything. What food we ate wouldn't have mattered at a different time. I had grown up eating everything and wasn't a picky eater, but I wasn't traveling alone; I was with Karen.

This was her first trip to Bujumbura. I wanted her first impression to be excellent, as if a poor first impression of where I was born was tantamount to a poor image of me. My insistence on weighing in or even paying for dinner had fallen on deaf ears—local hospitality obliged!

"Don't worry about it, Saba. I will tell you when you arrive," Babu had promised, which only made me worry more.

Babu is what I would call a stereotypical Burundian: laid-back, hospitable, with a great sense of humor and, almost always, a beer in hand.

"Listen, Saba!" Babu yelled on the phone, raising his voice above honking cars in the background. "Listen, I am on my way. We're going to Buyenzi for dinner!" He hung up the phone.

He's taking us to Buyenzi for dinner? That was precisely what I was worried about. Buyenzi is a less affluent neighborhood in the center of Bujumbura City. You don't go to Buyenzi if you're looking for high-end restaurants. You go there if you need to fix your car! The neighborhood is famous—or infamous, depending on personal experience—for its resourceful mechanics.

Babu arrived to pick us up at around 7:15 p.m., giving us a little time to shower and recover from the daylong trip. We got into the car as soon as he arrived and drove off.

On our way to the restaurant, Babu pointed at two buildings, the only ones whose height rose above two floors.

"Saba, do you remember the family that used to own this property?"

"No, I don't."

"So, the parents divorced after the man cheated on his wife. The separation forced them to sell the commercial buildings. But the kids are grown up now, so they're fine," he reassured me.

For Babu, life was simple like that; kids could simply outgrow the scars of a dysfunctional family.

I stared at the buildings and tried to recall their previous owner as we drove by, without success. Having Babu around was like having a private tour guide. In a way, he was doing by nature what I hoped to learn by profession.

The car drove to Buyenzi and made a sharp left down a narrow street dividing its rusty houses. We continued for a few more minutes until we lost sight of street lighting. Then Babu pulled the car over to the side of a road, where the curb would typically be.

The three of us walked through a narrow door and pushed through a bamboo-beaded curtain. The scent of spicy food and seasoning filled the restaurant's air. A few friends of Babu's sat in one corner, eating and drinking. They greeted us with excitement as soon as they saw Babu, who knew everyone in this town. He was like a celebrity, except he knew his fans by name.

Before we sat down, a restaurant attendant handed me a bar of soap and helped me wash my hands using water from a jar and a washbasin he had placed on the floor to collect used water. Karen and Babu did the same.

Then Karen and I went and took seats on opposite sides of the rectangular table next to Babu's friends. Shrinking candles distributed across the restaurant tables cast a yellow glow on the faces sitting around them. I sat on the wooden bench next to one of Babu's friends called Mutoka, short for Mutokambali, a Swahili name that means "one who comes from afar."

"Help yourselves, guys." Mutoka invited us to eat.

Our friends had ordered food before we arrived. I scooped a piece of hot ugali and dipped it into the sauce at the base of a ceramic bowl. A burning, earthy scent followed my hand to my mouth as I experienced the ugali's soft and heavy texture and savored its red-sauce coating. The spice inflamed my palate, but not so much that I had to fan my open mouth. I quickly swallowed the food.

The ugali was in the middle of the table, sitting on one big metal plate, while the sauce was in small ceramic bowls.

"Mutoka, what do you do for work?"

"Well, I work at a nearby church as a sound engineer," he said. "My job is part-time, though. They only need my services setting up the sound system on Sundays before church service and on Tuesdays and Saturdays for choir rehearsals."

"And does the church pay you for that?"

"No," he laughed. "They let me practice on their instruments. That's what I get. My goal is to study sound engineering in Nairobi one day. That's when I will make a living out of it."

His eyes lit up as he explained his career goals, and he seemed almost uninterested that the food at the table was running out. Everyone was eating from the same plate of ugali, and the small cassava dough hill was flattening at the speed of the fastest eaters.

The church is more than a spiritual community for many young people in Burundi; it's their hope of picking up a valuable craft that's otherwise too costly to nurture. Asking parents to pay for violin lessons or piano practice isn't an option for someone like Mutoka. I was glad that times were relatively peaceful in Burundi after the civil war had torn the country apart for over a decade. People were just getting the relative peace to be creative and think about their dreams and career goals.

Nations of the African Great Lakes region have had successive armed conflicts. War spread from country to country like a disease, gnawing at body parts one at a time.

When the Rwandan civil war and Tutsi genocide ended in 1994, Burundi and the DR Congo had their own civil wars, which raged in the second half of the 1990s. Successive conflicts wreaked havoc in the region, causing people to seek refuge across borders as war broke out in one country and relative peace returned to another.

Born in a refugee camp in neighboring Tanzania, he told me, Mutoka looked like a kid who had gone through a lot. A kid whom life had asked to be hopeful and "normal" despite a challenging up-bringing. I could relate to Mutoka's story, living in a refugee camp notwithstanding.

I, too, was born in a foreign land. Except that foreign land was this one. My parents were Rwandan refugees who had met and married in Bujumbura, where they had immigrated.

The 1994 genocide against the Tutsi was the culmination of a long campaign of ethnically motivated violence and persecution that started decades prior and forced many Tutsi into exile. From the early 1960s, to the 1970s–when my parents left Rwanda and settled in Burundi.

I grew up just like any other kid would. I didn't even know my parents were immigrants until my fifth-grade teacher gave us a home assignment in which we were to discuss where our parents had grown up. That was when my parents told me they came from a different country.

Since then, other kids would ask me why I didn't have an accent or when I would return home, even though Bujumbura was the only home I had known.

That said, we were the lucky ones. My siblings and I had a school, a home, and a city. A place that had welcomed my parents when they'd fled persecution in their homeland. I was grateful that my parents had had jobs, that we'd lived what you would call everyday life, and that this country had spared us the misery of growing up in a refugee camp. This is how most people cope with life's curveballs here. You don't complain and you don't cry, because there is always someone else who has it worse.

"Are you guys ready to go?" Babu interrupted the conversation.

I looked at Karen to check on her. She was leaning forward, absorbed in a conversation with another of Babu's friends. I looked at her and smiled, delighted that she, too, had enjoyed her company.

"I think we are," I said. "Thanks, Babu, this was a great idea!"

Humbled by this moment, I was glad Babu had taken us to this place and introduced us to his friends. The best dinner experience came not from the eccentric menu offerings of a fancy restaurant, but from a simple meal and the warmth of our company's welcome. Ultimately, it's not the place that matters; it's the company.

We bid adieu to the friends we met at the restaurant and hopped in our ride back to our hotel.

"Saba, are you sure you guys don't want to go clubbing?" Babu said.

"Maybe tomorrow."

The night was still young for Babu and his friends, but our earlier trip was weighing on my body. My eyes were heavy, and my attention was drifting.

Babu wasn't at the wheel this time. Instead of driving us back, he had convinced one of his friends to move us around.

As we left Buyenzi, our driver had an Amstel bottle between his legs, and he alternated between shifting gears and sipping beer. Babu, who sat in the front passenger seat, was holding a beer bottle as well; his hands wrapped around the beverage as if he were performing an exorcism over it. I looked at Karen, and we exchanged a smile upon realizing that they had relegated the only sober people in the car to the back seat!

o · o · o · o · o · o ·

WHEN I GOT TO MY bedroom, I couldn't find sleep even though my eyelids had been involuntarily closing on me when we'd left the restaurant. This was the first time I was back in Bujumbura in a long while. My childhood memories came back to mind. The wonderful memories, and then the rough ones.

When Rwanda was on the verge of genocide, Burundi's own

civil war was brewing. I remember my heart pounding fast and the terror of my ten-year-old self hearing gunfire for the first time, the deafening sound in my ears, the violence behind every shot. My brother and I would eat our meals beneath the table to avoid stray bullets. Even at that tender age, we had to learn what to do. When gunfire went off outside, we would dive underneath the table as if it were a horrifying game we played. Every sound of gunfire brought an angel of death, but somehow, we got used to it.

Age ten is when I lost my innocence. I saw a man being beaten to death for being in the wrong neighborhood. People ran after him, tackled him to the ground, and beat him up with bricks they had collected from a nearby construction site. I remember he knelt and pleaded for his life one last time before being struck into the afterlife by a metal bar. Before his killer hit his head, I looked away; before the full swing of his blow smacked his pleading head open. I ran home and didn't tell my mom or anyone else what I had just witnessed. I kept it to myself and didn't tell anyone until years later. His corpse lay lifeless on our street for two days, his hand clutching his gashed head. I never played on that street again.

My uncle Khivi lived with us at the time because his house was in the wrong neighborhood. At the dawn of the civil war in Burundi in the early 1990s, sporadic ethnic-based vigilante groups had segregated neighborhoods in Bujumbura. He was lucky, for he escaped an attempt on his life almost unscathed.

My uncle was crazy, but it somehow saved his life. When they came for him with guns and grenades one night, they fired warning shots from the compound outside his house to get him to come out. He pleaded with them to spare his soul. He gave them beer and asked them to leave him alone, but they wouldn't. He offered his fridge as ransom, but they refused. Desperate, he gave them his most prized possession: his video cassette player. But they declined! They wanted him dead. They wanted to take his life. When he realized that, he lost it! He started screaming and making babbling sounds. He stripped off his clothes, grabbed his deadly weapons, and came out running.

Stunned at what they saw, his detractors held their fire. He ran away completely naked, wielding a spear and a wooden shield!

He lived on baguettes and sugar water in our guest room. However, despite his odd personality, my younger brothers and I liked him. He had operated a makeshift movie theater business from his old house and had saved his two-piece aluminum trunk set full of VHS tapes before the detractors ransacked his house a few days after the incident. My uncle let us watch the few action movies in his stash that weren't R-rated.

As I recalled watching PG-rated action movies with my uncle, I finally nodded off...

Back to Ngagara

o·o·o·o·o·o·o·o·o·o·o·o·o·o·o·o·o·o·o·o·

I drove south toward Ngagara in the morning. The sun was high and not a single cloud was up. Karen was in the passenger seat next to me, wearing a low-cut black-and-white kitenge dress and sunglasses. Sunrays lit up her skin tone in a bronze glow, as if she had handpicked the perfect tan from the color palette of graphic design software. Under the sunlight coming in through the windshield and the car window, her hair color turned from dirty blond to pure blond.

Coming back to this city after a long time brought back more childhood memories. I wanted to return to where I had grown up, meet my childhood friends, and sit on the wooden benches of my old elementary school once again.

Humid air pushed against the car with a humming noise and hit our faces through lowered windows.

Like everything else in my old neighborhood, houses looked smaller than I remembered. Strange looks had replaced what used to be familiar faces at every street corner.

After making several stops to ask for directions, I parked the old Nissan Datsun, which I had borrowed from my friend Babu, near my elementary school. I wiped my brow with my forearm as I pulled up to a deserted school.

Sweat dripped from my body, staining my striped white shirt. Humid weather, coupled with the exercise of turning the rugged mechanical steering wheel, triggered profuse sweating.

Bujumbura lies on the plains of the Rusizi River, which flows from Lake Kivu into Lake Tanganyika. Compared to the rest of the country, the weather is hot and damp.

I stepped out of the car, and not a soul was in sight except a guard and two boys kicking a ball made of plastic bags. I left the car and paced toward what used to be my fifth-grade classroom.

Bushes had invaded the area, erasing every marked boundary from what used to be our football field. Roof tiles looked darker than I recalled; they had adopted a dusky shade under the weight of passing years. A massive cell tower, a rare sign of modern infrastructure, dominated the blue sky and stood over the grounds where we used to host the school fair.

Memories of my first school play came back to me. I could still feel the piercing, angry look my childhood friend Landry had given me the day I'd stolen his line during a performance in front of our parents. He never forgave me for it.

"Quand tu fumes, le bébé fume aussi," I whispered again as I stood on the dirt ground where the stage had been. I remembered the line I had stolen from Landry but still had no recollection of what I was supposed to say before Landry's turn in the act. To this day, I still can't remember what my line was. The only memory I had was that of me wagging my finger at the stuffed belly of our friend Maggie, saying, "When you smoke, the baby smokes too."

Caught by surprise, Landry had stood speechless for a while, not knowing what to say, before stuttering through the same line again.

Karen walked next to me, following me with both interest and amusement. She was discovering where I'd come from, where I'd grown up as a kid, and I loved it. I wanted to share my story with her. My life, too.

My hand dipped through a broken window of the building, and the delicate strings of cobwebs trapped my hand, jealously guarding the school against outside intruders. I shoved the cobwebs aside and peeked inside.

Benches unevenly arranged in rows furnished the classroom. A cracked blackboard had turned gray and looked like it hadn't seen a lesson in a long time. A tube lamp hung from the ceiling with wires sticking out. Part of the roof had collapsed. Only the dark blue metal doors were still intact; they were secured with a padlock.

"What happened here?" I turned to the guard, who had followed us, visibly bewildered by the curious visitors. "I used to live here. I used to go to this school," I said, clarifying the backstory.

"They turned this school into a refugee camp a while ago," he explained. "Maybe you should help rebuild it if you went here."

"How would I help, my friend? I don't have the resources to do so," I said. "It's sad to see my school in a dilapidated condition."

My eyes took another look through the window, and I couldn't help but remember my old classmates and Mr. Rusa, my fifth-grade teacher. He would stand in front of his class with perfect posture, repeating his favorite words of wisdom in French: Le temps perdu ne reviendra jamais; "lost time never comes back."

The Shores of Lake Tanganyika

o·o·o·o·o·o·o·o·o·o·o·o·o·o·o·o·o·o·o·

A small fence about six feet tall encircled a bask of crocodiles. The wire mesh erected on a mold-covered foundation was the only barrier separating the predators from the visitors at the Musée Vivant Zoo. A small pond of greenish water cradled the crocodiles as they lay immobile, faking death to trick gullible prey. Their osteoderm-covered skin was almost indistinguishable from the dirt underneath them.

We wandered along a path invaded by wild grass and intermittently cut by trees that had sprung throughout the premises unplanned and provided a lovely shade from the afternoon heat. A sign hung on one building and read Maison des Serpents, or "snake house" in French.

In addition to their native languages, African countries speak the language of their former colonial occupants. Burundi was part of Deutsch-Ostafrika, a German colony that stretched from Lake

Tanganyika eastward, all the way to the Indian Ocean. This territory covered modern-day Rwanda, Burundi, and Tanzania. The French language derives from Belgium's cultural influence. The defeat of the Germans during World War I resulted in German colonies being divided up among the victors. Belgium inherited present-day Rwanda and Burundi, while Britain gained control of Tanzania.

Karen and I took a self-guided tour and walked around the building, admiring the venomous reptiles secured behind glass walls. When we reached the end corner of the exhibition house, we noticed a broken glass wall. The cell had no snake inside, but it still had a label taped on top that read Vipère du Sahara, which means "Sahara viper."

"A snake is missing here." Karen pointed at the empty cell.

"I think we should get out of here," I said. "You don't want to be trapped in this building with a missing viper."

Karen and I quietly made our way toward the exit and walked to Lake Tanganyika. The beach was within walking distance, and the heat and humidity in the air made for perfect weather for an afternoon at the beach.

Hotels, restaurants, and beach resorts lined up alongside the lakeshore. The wind whistled over the lake, sending waves splattering on the sandy shore where naked kids were swimming next to a few women in black one-piece bathing suits.

Eager to get into the water, Karen removed her flip-flops and carried them in her hands to move faster and allow her feet to kiss the ground. We headed toward the pulsing waves, tottering through the shifting sand underneath our feet.

"Karen, I'll go get us snacks. Do you need anything?"

Karen threw her backpack down and ran toward the lake. She looked back and smiled at me, defying me to catch her in a race. I let her put some distance between us before springing after her in a flash. Realizing that we'd left her backpack behind unattended, I immediately applied the brakes. I conceded defeat and turned back to pick up her bag and buy snacks while she went into the water.

Wind from the lake blew against my face with a rustling noise. Sand slipped through my toes, spreading the heat it had collected through constant exposure to the sun to my feet. I found a quiet spot at the beach past the Blue Bay resort and the famous Hôtel Club du Lac Tanganyika.

I half-buried two water bottles I had in the sand and carefully put my bag of grilled sleek lates next to me.

Karen was a stone's throw from me, frolicking on the lakeshore. As small waves hit her ankles, she splashed the shallow waters with her feet. The wind blew through her curly hair as she ran around with her arms spread, hoping to generate enough lift force to fly away. I wondered where Karen would go if she could fly. Would she come back for me?

Lake Tanganyika has been a popular getaway for locals and foreigners for decades. Throughout history, it's been the envy of explorers, guerrilla fighters, and wildlife enthusiasts. If this lake could talk, it would have a lot to say.

On the shores of Lake Tanganyika, journalist Henry Morton Stanley said the famous words, "Dr. Livingstone, I presume?" after he found the stranded Christian missionary and explorer in 1871. Here, on the southern shore of this lake, primatologist Jane Goodall conducted her famous work and research on wild chimpanzees. Even Che Guevara, the Marxist revolutionary, stayed by this lake in 1965 during his failed attempt to bring the Communist revolution to the Congo. No wonder the lake exudes a mystical aura that makes one feel as if they are part of a bigger story.

Karen stood away, facing the sunset across the lake at the edge of splashing waves. The setting sun cast a shadow on the figurine she had made in the sand behind her. Her curves fit perfectly in the sapphire bikini she was wearing.

I looked down and ran my hand through my Afro hair in a nervous gesture when I saw Karen heading back in my direction. She collected her dress off the ground and walked up to me as I struggled to keep my eyes off her body.

At this moment, I realized the impression Karen had made on me went deeper than my long hair and forgone mustache—a look she was rather fond of.

"Hey, you okay? You didn't swim at all." Karen reached for a towel in her backpack next to me.

"I'm good. Just taking in the moment and enjoying the sunset."

"Should we head home? It's getting dark outside," she said.

I extended my right hand in her direction for her to pull me up. Basketball manners had stuck with me since I'd played for my high school team. Every time I hit the floor, I feel like I'm in a basketball game; I wait for a teammate to help me up.

Soon enough, I would find out whether Karen would hold my heart as kindly as she held my hand.

We strolled past the Bora Bora resort after stopping in the showers so Karen could change clothes. I stood outside the changing rooms, looking at two kids playing beach volleyball outside. They had changed the rules when their friends left, only throwing the ball back and forth over a net planted in the sand.

○ · ○ · ○ · ○ · ○ · ○ ·

THE LAKE BECAME A DARK silver shade as scudding clouds invaded the sky, and the last sunrays flashed their goodbyes over raised mountains across the lake.

While we walked on the beach, we stumbled upon what looked like a pop-up dance party.

Burundi had gone through tough times, but war never stopped people from having fun here. In fact, at night it was common to hear both sporadic gunfire and loud music from nearby clubs at the same time!

Karen and I stood by at first, shy but interested and observant. We watched the group of people dancing to the rhythm of a Latin beat until one of them waved at us to join them on the dance floor. The dancing faces were glowing with excitement, the reflection of string lights on their sweating foreheads.

Without hesitation, Karen leaped onto the dance floor, extending her arms toward me. They were playing salsa music. I wrapped my right arm around her shoulder blades in a close body position. While planning the next spin move, I silently counted the steps in my head. I kept it simple and stuck to movements I knew: cross-body lead, left turn, an "enchufla double," and then the initial steps.

To the soothing voice and rhythmic drum, we danced. Karen's confidence on the dance floor shone brightly, a trait I had never seen before. She had a strong, pleasant presence. She got lost in music as if nothing else mattered and no one else was watching her. Her natural curves exaggerated her hip movements and style of dancing. She threw her arms in the air as she spun, her dress swinging and flashing her thighs, in perfect tune with the pulsing song.

As the song neared its last notes, I threw Karen's right arm over my shoulder, held her back with my right arm, and dipped her gently. Smiling, Karen trapped my face with her left hand and looked at me to execute the dip move and drop her frame into my arm. She looked at me as if she could read my every thought through the iris of my eye. She had read what I wanted to do. In dance, just like in life, Karen could read me well.

Lights around the circular bungalow and surrounding the dance floor shone with a feeble glow, like a fading candle. Still, the absence of light pollution provided a clear night for viewing the stars.

Music and chatter from the dancing crowd faded behind us as we strolled along the crunching sand back to our hotel. We had stopped dancing, but Karen was still holding my hand.

"Hey, I wanted to talk to you about something," I said, swinging her hand a bit for attention. She paused for a few seconds before she answered.

"What?" she said, her head facing down.

"About that kiss," I said. "We never got to talk about it."

"What about it?" she asked.

"I think I like you, Karen!"

"You think?" she gibed, trying to buy herself time to think about an answer.

"Well, you know what I mean," I said. "Would you . . . like to go out with me?"

Karen paused. She looked at me, then at her feet sifting through the sand in the dark.

"Please, say something!"

"Oh, Saba. I don't know."

"What do you mean, you don't know?"

"I kissed you in the moment, you know," she said.

"It was a wonderful moment, though, wasn't it?"

"Yes, it was, but . . ."

"Well, I thought I made you happy, and I know you make me happy!" I said, letting go of her hand.

"It's not that," she said. "I'm really not looking for a relationship."

"Come on! Let's give us a chance!" I said, almost in denial about what was unfolding before my eyes.

If the bonding, the sensual dancing, and the weekend getaway by the lake don't set me up for a yes, then nothing will!

Her answer felt so wrong, like a bad ending to a good movie.

"I don't know, Saba."

"All right! I get it!"

The splashing waves of the lake sounded a little louder, even as we walked away from them toward the main road to get a taxi home.

"I didn't say no, you know?" Karen muttered after a moment.

"What? I'm confused."

"All I'm saying is, not now."

"So, it's not a yes, but it's not a no either?"

"I need some time to sort myself out ..."

"How much time?"

"Look, I just came out of an unhealthy relationship, and I'm on a dating hiatus for two years before I can date again," she said.

"What? You seriously want me to wait for two years?"

"I'm so sorry, Saba," she said. "I know it's not fair."

"First, that's unreasonable to ask of anyone," I said in an aggravated voice. "Second, that sounds arbitrary. Why not three years? Or one year, seven months, and two days?"

"That's not funny, Saba!"

"You can make it today, as far as I'm concerned."

"Please, stop! I don't want to get mad at you right now."

"Sorry! I don't mean to be insensitive, but two years? C'mon, why can't we be together right now?"

"Look, I really like you, Saba, but I don't want to be pressured into a new relationship right now." Karen brushed her hand across her eyes, which were glowing in the dark. We were now standing by the side of the road near the beach resorts, waiting to hail a ride home.

A few cars whooshed by on the dark road.

"Hey, no pressure!" I wrapped my arms around her in a side hug. "Listen, take the time you need. I'll be here when you're ready, okay?" Karen agreed with a nod of her head.

"You have to promise you will be my travel partner in the meantime."

Rambling, I said anything to change the subject and stop Karen from crying, to avoid having to explain to the cab driver why the girl I was riding home with at night was in tears.

"Promise!" Karen said.

We finally identified a passing Toyota Corolla cab by its glowing yellow Taxi sign fitted on its roof.

"I have something I want to tell you, too," Karen said as soon as we settled in the back seat.

"Oh God! Is it good news, or will I get my heart broken again?" I said, exasperated.

"It's good news. Well, I think." Karen grimaced.

"What is it?"

"I told you I was job searching, right? Well, I got a job offer."

"That's great news! Congratulations!"

"It won't be in Kigali, though," she said. "So, you may not like that."

"Where is it?"

"It's in Zambia. I'll move there soon."

"Hey, I'm happy for you. I was praying for Kigali just so we could stay together, but Zambia isn't that far away. When did you find out?"

"A couple of days ago."

One of Those Days

aba. Sabaaa!" Mr. Sadiki yelled across the adjacent room, forgoing the office phone to use his thundering voice.

Everything seemed a bit more chaotic that day. That morning I had hit the snooze button on my phone fifteen times before I'd finally rolled out of bed to get ready for work. I had traded breakfast for more sleep time and was running on a couple cups of black coffee from the drip coffee machine at the office.

The fatigue of a long weekend trip had kicked in. The roaring noises of diesel engines outside our office tested my patience. The Monday morning action was full-on, and drivers were preparing to take tourists to their respective destinations.

Despite a welcome-branded doormat at the entrance, my office building had an unwelcoming look. The few pictures pinned to a wide wooden board showing tour guides and tourists on safaris were the exception. Everything else looked bland. Office desks were beige, the window curtains were light brown, and the floor tiles were gray.

Albert Baho, my colleague, nicknamed AB, looked at me with a smile as soon as he heard Mr. Sadiki shouting my name. I rolled back my office chair, hurriedly took another sip from my coffee mug, and almost spilled it on my white shirt. I stormed out of my office to meet my boss, Albert looking on as if the entire scene was for his amusement.

"What?" I said to AB, before walking out of our shared office to see my boss next door. It was one of those mornings when you don't want to talk to anyone. When you hope no one will make demands of you for the day. But I knew that wouldn't happen.

"Good morning, sir!" I greeted my boss as soon as I stepped into his office.

"Take a seat, my friend!" he said. "I was reading our quarterly sales report, and it doesn't look good. We need a strategy to diversify our portfolio."

I listened and scribbled words on my notepad with forced attention.

"Where are you on your new package proposal?" He stared at me from above the frames of his low-hanging glasses.

"I reached out to regional airlines for discounted deals, but I'm still waiting to hear from them."

"I really want you to work faster, Saba! Or we're gonna have to part ways!" He paused, then said, "I want you to think out of the box too!" He raised his eyebrows in a V shape, drawing wrinkles on his shiny bald head. My heart pounded fast, but I kept my calm and listened.

"Do you think you can do that?" he said with skepticism.

"Of course, sir!"

"That's why I hired you, to be honest. I knew you had no experience as a tour agent. But I wanted someone who could be resourceful and eventually grow into a strategy and planning role. Why don't you consider deals in Asia or Europe too in your search? We should aim for a global market," he barked before smacking the papers he was holding on his office desk.

I squinted, suddenly more concerned that his spit would touch my face. However, he took care of his hygiene; I could smell the fresh mint from his mouth as he yelled.

Mr. Sadiki had decorated his office in a rudimentary fashion. No family photographs or paintings hung on the blank walls of his office. Only a wooden shelf full of company reports and travel magazines stood on the small ledge to his left.

A massive pile of documents from the finance office lay in a binder on the table, awaiting his signature. A small metal trophy with the words Employee of the Year Award engraved at the base sat lonely on the shelf. It looked like the only validation he'd ever received in his life. He had earned the award from a previous job.

Mr. Sadiki had founded MBT when he'd grown impatient to make his own mark on the blossoming tourism industry. He had worked for another travel agency for ten years before starting his own company. He longed to make a name for himself and add a few awards to his meager trophy collection.

Rwanda is a landlocked country, at least a thousand kilometers away from the nearest coastline, the gateway to the world market. Because of this, the government enacted policies and measures meant to diversify its export portfolio and encourage a service- and knowledge-based economy. The tourism industry was now on track to beat coffee and tea as Rwanda's top foreign exchange earner. Mr. Sadiki was one of several entrepreneurs capitalizing on this business environment.

I tried to peek through the sales report that was so aggravating to Mr. Sadiki, but I couldn't see.

"Here! Take it and see for yourself." He handed me the piece of paper, feeding my curiosity. I studied at the report and the drawn graph in the middle representing the company sales curve. I could read that sales were still increasing, but at a lower rate.

"Please take it and read it! It will provide a context for your work. Come to me when you are done with a new expansion package proposal," he ordered.

I left Mr. Sadiki's office, my eyes fixed on the report, still disturbed by his tone of voice. His autocratic side and threat of firing me took me aback. There was a lot I still didn't understand about this company and its leadership, which bothered me. Uncertainty can be the most uncomfortable feeling. I didn't know my boss well enough to tell if this behavior was in character for him and if I could work and thrive in this environment. I didn't know if I could put up with it—assuming I didn't get fired first.

Mr. Sadiki, a middle-aged and divorced man, was an odd personality. He would always insist on being called Mr. Sadiki. Despite his idiosyncrasies, he worked hard and led by example. He always came to the office early and left late, after everyone else did. Whether this was because of his work ethic or because he didn't have a life outside the office, I didn't know. He worked on weekends, too, on occasion.

"So, you got yelled at too, huh?" Albert said when I returned to my office, visibly rattled.

". . . And you didn't bother to tell me what would happen?"

"Aw, don't take it personally," he said with a condescending tone. "Everyone gets yelled at by the boss at least once."

Pressure and defiance have been motivating factors for me since childhood. I've been feeding off them since my middle school classmate, Nadine Bwenge, challenged my learning abilities. "You cannot outperform me in class," she would tell me. Nadine was one of those students who insisted we have homework every day and reminded the teacher whenever she would forget to give us an assignment.

I got my revenge when I collected the third-place transcript on our grade's proclamation day while she waited in a corner with her mom for fifth place to be called.

The education system was such that kids wouldn't know how they did until the semester ended, when the school would publicly rank them from first to last. This was, of course, a guaranteed source of anxiety or, for the lucky few, of pride for awaiting kids and parents. Some suspecting parents would even bring a cane to the ceremony just in case. They chased their kids and spanked them in front of the entire gathering upon hearing about their poor classroom performance, much to their children's chagrin and everybody else's laughter!

"What are you smiling about?" Albert said, surprised at the grin on my face as I mused about my middle school drama.

"Nothing!" I wiped it off and jotted down a few ideas from my conversation with Mr. Sadiki into my notebook.

The company might fire me and force me to start over again. I sat at my desk, perplexed. I wasn't ready to move to a different job. Mr. Sadiki's comments made me doubt further that I was ready for this type of work. More than anything, however, I resented Albert's mercenary-like attitude. He had known our boss could be short-tempered and hadn't warned me about it. I was still relatively new at the company, while he had worked here for quite some time.

It seemed like I was experiencing middle school drama with my classmates again, a zero-sum game. Me being third in class meant that everybody else would lose that position. Albert's gesture betrayed a team spirit—the hallmark of a healthy work environment.

The Setback

o·o·o·o·o·o·o·o·o·o·o·o·o·o·o·o·o·o·o·

What's up, Dan?" I answered the phone and paused the movie playing on my computer screen. I had left the office earlier than usual that day, promptly packing my backpack when the clock hit 5:00 p.m.

"How are you? How was your trip with Karen?"

"Dan, hold on a bit!" I stood up from the bed, pulled the curtain back, and closed the metal-framed window in my room. Mosquitoes disturbed the sense of rest in my bedroom at night. Like thieves, they too strike when the sun goes down. I had a mosquito net hanging over my bed, but it didn't protect me from their whining noise at night or their bites, which caused itchy bumps in the morning. It was an old mosquito net I'd inherited from my sister when I'd moved out of my parents' house after college. Somehow, mosquitoes could still find the three coin-sized holes on the net, sneak through at night, and feast on me while I slept.

"Hey, sorry about that. My window was open," I said as I sat back on my bed. "The trip with Karen was great. We went to Tanganyika beach and saw my old elementary school."

"And?" Dan said.

"And what?"

"C'mon! You went on a weekend trip with her. Just the two of you!" he emphasized. "Something had to have happened, right?"

"Well, that part didn't go as expected," I said with a forced smile.

"Did you ask her out?"

"I did, but you won't believe what she told me."

"C'mon, spill the beans!" he said, as excited to learn about my adventure as a kid who wanted to hear his favorite bedtime story.

"Don't get too excited. It's not a happy ending," I said, tempering expectations. "She said she's not ready now but will be in two years."

"Wait, what? No way! For real?"

"Yep! That was my reaction too . . . well, sort of!"

"Dude, forget about her!" Dan said with his imposing voice. "That's a code word for 'I'm not interested.' You know that, right?"

"Why would Karen talk to me in codes, though?"

"She's a girl! All girls talk in codes," he said before interrupting his own train of thought. "Wait, don't tell me you're actually considering waiting for her for two years?"

"Maybe." I rubbed my blurry eyes and switched the phone to my left ear.

"Oh, Saba. Don't do it."

"I thought about it, and the thing is—I like her, okay!"

"I'm sure she said that because she didn't want to hurt your feelings with an outright rejection."

"Well, that ship has sailed," I said. "To add to that, I had a really long day at work today." I adjusted my bed pillow to better support my back, leaning against the headboard and the wall. "Except for that part, it was a beautiful trip. I got to see my old friend and visit my old neighborhood."

"Seriously, I think you should move on," Dan insisted.

"You think?"

"I mean, why in the name of sanity would you put your life on hold for two years waiting for a girl who's not even interested?"

"I don't know, Dan! I think she likes my company, and—"

"Of course she does!" Dan interrupted. "It's a convenient relationship for her. It doesn't mean she's into you. Girls do that shit all the time. They'll stick you in the friend zone and do everything with you except date you. Which is what you want, right?"

My fingers ran through my hair as my body pushed an exasperated sigh through my cell phone's microphone.

I struggled to explain why I thought there could be something between Karen and me. It wasn't the words she'd said to me, for there was nothing said to that effect. Rather, it was something nonverbal, something subtle, romantic. It was the way she would warmly tap on my shoulder in conversations, her laughs at my stupid jokes, her gentle rubs on my back, or hugs held for too long.

The night we returned from our weekend trip, our cab driver first dropped Karen off at her house. She hugged me goodbye. After stepping out of the car, she held on to the door for a couple of seconds as if she had forgotten something. Then she rushed back inside and hugged me again, a little tighter this time. After that, she exited the taxicab, threw her backpack over her shoulder, and kept eye contact with me until the cab drove away.

"Look, a lot is going on in my life right now," I said in a resolute tone. "I need a moment to process everything. We'll see what happens. How's Elise doing?"

"She's cool," Dan said of his girlfriend.

"She didn't ask you to wait before you guys were together, did she?" I smiled.

"Nah, she knew I would have moved on in a heartbeat."

"Some girls take time to decide, you know."

"Or they're not interested! Besides, girls like men who have options."

"Well, that's your opinion. Maybe she's thinking about it, which, frankly, I find attractive. It means she's not easy."

"That's not how it works . . ."

By the time I got off the phone with Dan, I was lying on the side of my squeaky bed with my feet hanging down and touching the cement floor in my bedroom. My hand holding the phone had collapsed on my head, and the socks did little to isolate my feet from the cold floor.

My window was dark, hidden behind pleated curtains. The lightbulb on the ceiling and a bright computer screen lit up my room, but it wasn't the same as having pure sunlight. The unnatural light painted everything in my room a yellowish hue.

Like the proverbial Sword of Damocles, life felt like an elusive quest for happiness. I knew joy was near, but I couldn't quite reach it yet. Not too long ago, I thought I had solved two of the most essential things in a man's life: following a dream career and finding love. I had a new job I was excited about and a romantic beach get-away planned with Karen. Now my boss doubted my competence at work, and I had yet to win Karen's heart.

Our house gate creaked open, the loud noise tearing through the quiet evening. A car pulled into the garage. Its laser-like beams shone through my window and quickly passed across my room before dying down shortly after the driver turned off the car engine.

I immediately stood up and wiped tears off my face. My bedroom door was unlocked, and my roommate's concept of hospitality trumped any notion of personal space. Kamana always said hello when he saw the light behind my window curtains or underneath my room's door.

CHAPTER 3

The Farewell Dinner

O·O·O·O·O·O·O·O·O·O·O·O·O·O·O·O·O·O·O·O·

"One, two, one, two . . . check, check!" the band's lead singer thundered through the loudspeakers fitted around the bar area on the lower floor.

The evening wind was blowing through the thatched-roof bar, providing the perfect temperature—not too cold or hot and just about the right amount of humidity. A tonic water bottle sat lonely on the white wooden table before me. Kigali's rolling hills could be seen in the distance, fading behind one another and gracefully disappearing over the horizon as the falling dusk dimmed the day. Since it was dark enough outside, the convention center, Kigali's landmark building, flashed green, light blue, and yellow in the sky.

Carved masks, a map of Africa, and matching zebra paintings decorated the black-and-white-themed bar. A wooden staircase led to the balcony where I sat with a view of the pool below. At the entrance of the bar, called Pili Pili, was a large portrait depicting three blue-vested people on their motorbike taxis—a standard mode of public transportation in Kigali.

Pili Pili, the word for "hot pepper" in Swahili, is the hottest bar in town. I had handpicked the venue for Karen's farewell dinner. The place fills up quickly in the evenings, so I'd arrived early to secure a table for the group. I was proud that I had planned ahead. My table location was perfect—or it would have been if not for the smell of cigarette smoke from people sitting nearby.

The weather allowed me to wear a T-shirt that night, which I regretted as soon as mosquitoes bit my arms.

Wooden shades covered the main lamps hanging from the ceiling, which cast small penumbras on the vast balcony. The lights barely provided enough visibility to see the people around me.

Around seven, Karen showed up. Her distinct walk set her apart from an almost indistinguishable crowd congregating at the bar's entrance. I stood and waved in her direction, which she noticed when she got to the top of the stairs.

"You look great," I said, planting a kiss on her right cheek to greet her.

Shortly after Karen arrived, the band started playing, as if we had all been waiting in unison for the guest of honor to arrive.

Karen was wearing a blue satin dress. Her face glowed from lip gloss and makeup. She had applied discreet eyeliner, harnessing her naturally symmetrical facial features.

"Good choice on the bar." Karen smiled as she pulled a chair next to me.

"Pulling the big guns for you tonight, you know!"

"I can see that!"

"Welcome to Pili Pili!" the server said with a distinct Rwandan accent. He put the drinks menu on our table before quickly disappearing to attend to the next table.

"Are you all packed and ready?" I said about her imminent relocation.

"Yeah, mostly," Karen said, her attention distracted by the pool.

The blue pool was empty and still but for an inflatable ring floating on the surface, giving the optical illusion of levitating.

"I don't know if I told you this, but my company has been looking into expanding activities to other countries, and Zambia is one of them," I said.

"Look, Elise and Dan are here," Karen said, triggering my head to look where she was pointing.

As if to circle back to where it had all begun, I had invited Dan and Elise to join the dinner, reuniting the initial crew that had made the trek to Virunga.

"Great to see you guys," I greeted Dan and Elise.

Dan grabbed the back of a chair, which had just been vacated at a nearby table, and dragged it next to the group to add a fourth seat.

"I love this place!" Dan said with a loud and enthusiastic voice over the sound of music and bar noise.

"I know, right?" Karen yelled, trying to match Dan's energy. "I said the same to Saba." She smiled at me.

Karen and I had this thing going for a while where I would pick restaurants and she would decide what we ate on nights out.

"Karen, Zambia is so dope!" Dan said excitedly. "You have to check out Victoria Falls and go swim in the 'devil's pool'! It's the most epic thing I've done! You feel the force of the water pushing your body to a sheer drop down the waterfall, only to be held back by a rock lip at the edge."

The crowd gathered around the bar entrance on the lower level burst into a loud *ooh*. Manchester United was playing West Ham on TV.

The English Premier League has a massive following in the region. The top teams, commonly known as the Big Four—Manchester United, Arsenal, Chelsea, and Liverpool—command an army of hard-core fans who never miss a game of their favorite football team, no matter who they play.

"I'm really looking forward to it," Karen said, brushing her arms to chase away mosquitoes.

"You can go bungee jumping, too! Zambia is like an adrenaline junkie's paradise," Dan said. Elise, who was sitting next to him, rolled her eyes. She gave him that look that said he was full of it.

"Babe, you refused to go jump with me!" Dan apologetically pulled Elise toward her and kissed her forehead.

"You know I'm afraid of heights!" Elise turned to me and Karen. "Do you guys know what he did when we visited Zambia?" she said, pleading her case with us. "He left me at the hostel and went bungee jumping with his ex-girlfriend, whom we met there." Elise shook her head, swinging her ponytail, which slicked her red hair away from her face.

"He did?" Karen said, amused.

"She is not my ex-girlfriend!" Dan said. "Look, we ran into an old friend of mine at the hostel, and she happened to be going bungee jumping too."

"A 'friend.'" Elise gestured with her index fingers.

"Okay, I drunkenly hooked up with her once back in the day, but it was nothing serious, I promise!" Dan said.

"Whatever!" Elise said.

"Are you guys good?" the server said, carrying a Primus-branded tray in his left hand with an empty glass atop it.

Musicians onstage on the floor below, opposite the swimming pool, played M'bilia Bel's classic "Nakei Nairobi," or "I am going to Nairobi."

Nairobi is a metropolitan city full of transplants from across East Africa. Many young people dream of making it big under the bright lights of her entrepreneurial spirit. She attracts a particular type of people: People whose hometowns are too small for their dreams. People who aren't afraid to leave friends and family behind, who pack their bags and move in a hopeless quest to make a difference in the world and better their careers.

I watched the band and tuned out as Karen chatted with Dan and Elise. Even though I feared that living apart meant growing apart, I wanted to support Karen and help her transition into her new job.

Like a dancer who reluctantly lets go of his ballerina's hand in a dance routine, I had to let go of her. But Karen moving away felt like losing a piece of myself. The worst part was that I didn't know what to do about it. I was unsure how I would see her again. I wanted to ask her to decline her job offer and stay with me. That last thought was desperate, so I kept it close to my heart and didn't voice it to her. I knew she would have said that it was an irrational demand, that it was so 1968, a selfish move. That said, the thought crossed my mind because, to me, finding a new job was easier than finding a new lover—at least one I felt this strongly about.

My car was at the mechanic's garage, so Karen got a ride home from Dan and Elise after dinner at Pili Pili. I took a motorbike taxi home.

I waved at one of the two motorbike taxis parked outside Pili Pili and put on the helmet as the motorcycle roared away. About a twenty-minute walk from my place, I convinced the driver to drop me off by the roadside so I could walk the rest of the way.

When I arrived at the cobblestone road near the Kigali Convention Center, traffic had receded. The night was serene, almost devoid of car engine noises, human noises, or any noise, except for a couple of motorcycles driving by.

I strolled downhill toward my neighborhood, keeping my feet on the sidewalk despite the empty road. I had walked this path countless times before, so often that I could still find my way home blindfolded. It was dark out, but I could picture where each brick house lining the cobblestone road was. I knew where they stood; I could tell their patterns and colors apart. No one else was walking outside that night, which was unusual, but I had a feeling that someone was watching me from a window. Houses were all too close to the sidewalk that, as an afterthought, the city's public works had carved out of people's front yards.

The bar vibe and the band had left a melancholic feeling in me. Soon Karen would live in a different city, and I didn't like it. I resented how the cosmic powers had allowed me to meet Karen and love her so much, only to have her disappear to a distant land so quickly. Imagine how different my life would have been had Karen said yes when I'd asked her out in Bujumbura. I already had our lives planned out. We would have looked for jobs in the same city.

Or, if she wouldn't, I was ready to be the one to move; maybe I could have done some marketing work remotely for MBT. Or perhaps I would have found another job. We would have rented a house with a big yard and a big dog—a German shepherd, to be specific. I'd grown up around dogs as a kid and have always wanted my children to grow up the same.

But as I approached my house, I felt as if I were waking up from a happy dream, unable to hold on to the good feeling because the ideal life I imagined wasn't the reality of my life. The reality was that I was coming home to an empty house. I lived with a houseboy and a roommate, but I barely saw them, except on weekends. My roommate, Kamana, and I had different schedules most days. Besides, he had been dating this girl for six months, which meant marriage was around the corner. It's common for Christians in the mold of Kamana to get married after dating for only a year or less. With sex before marriage off the table, they naturally shorten the waiting time lest they live in sin. Before long, he would move out, and I would go through the hassle, once again, of finding a new roommate or another apartment.

As I got closer to my house, past a popular neighborhood bar called Le Grenier, "the attic" in French, the street got noisier. People were sitting on the patio outside the bar drinking beer when I walked by. There was another bar not that far away. Still, people sat on stools by the sidewalk outside the popular bar rather than sitting comfortably in the less popular one for reasons that puzzled me. They both served the same beer brands, but people would flock to one and completely ignore the other.

o · o · o · o · o · o ·

I REACHED INTO MY POCKET and found my house keys, then opened the squeaky front door of our house. Kamana was home this time, sitting in the living room with his long limbs extended on the table. He held a book called *God's Undertaker: Has Science Buried God?* by John C. Lennox. The red light on the surge protector was still on, and a game controller sat near the TV table.

Kamana was an intriguing personality. His two hobbies were video games and Christianity. If he wasn't reading the Bible or some Christian book, you would find him playing *Street Fighter* or *Naruto* on the television.

"Hey, bro! How are you?" Kamana said, removing his reading glasses.

"Good! How are you?" I retreated to my room without waiting for an answer.

With a loud drop, I threw my backpack on the floor next to my bedside table. I changed into my sleeping clothes: black sweatpants and an MBT T-shirt I had received at my job orientation. I had worn it once during the event and later decided I should wear it only inside my house. The T-shirt had the acronym MBT in green Trebuchet typeface atop a gray background.

Although we worked in the service industry, Mr. Sadiki was not keen on investing in quality swag. He had bought a stack of ugly T-shirts at a bargain and decided, against everybody's opinion, that we should go through them all before purchasing new ones.

A few minutes later, Kamana came knocking on my bedroom door. I was lying on my bed, ready to binge-watch a show on my computer.

"Hey, dinner is ready," he said. His subtle way of asking me to sit at the dining table and eat together.

Like most people in this part of the world, we had a live-in salaried houseboy who would cook meals and clean the house for us.

Meat sauce, white rice, Irish potatoes, and vegetables mixed with black beans . . . I opened and checked every casserole wearing my grumpy face before taking a seat at the table across from Kamana.

As he finished setting the table, the houseboy brought the last dinner serving: a flask full of black tea. He put it on the table next to the white ceramic sugar container and left the room. His key chain scratched against the metal door as he locked the back entrance with a clattering noise and retreated to his back room.

After putting food on his plate, Kamana joined his hands and placed his elbows on the table's surface, his faith firmly planted in Christ. He prayed over his meal, eyes shut like always before dinner.

I had grown up Christian myself—more of a de facto Catholic, I should say. Where I'm from, if you're not religious and someone asks, you say you're Catholic.

The Catholic Church has influenced Rwandan culture and tradition ever since Franco-German Bishop Jean-Joseph Hirth established the first Roman Catholic mission in southern Rwanda at the dawn of the twentieth century. You can find the influence of Christianity all over the nation, in the architecture of church buildings towering over towns across the land, in local folklore, and in language. For example, the local word for "first name" translates as "Christian name," from the Catholic tradition of newborn babies getting their first names during baptism. Even though I hadn't seen the inside of a church building in several years, I claimed adherence to Catholicism because I have a first name. I have always gone by my last name, Saba, however.

Kamana was a member of one of the more outspoken Protestant churches. Many gained popularity after the Tutsi genocide of 1994, attracting a younger crowd through their fiery preachers and rock bands. Such church services provided a lively and more attractive alternative to the solemn Catholic worship service.

Kamana was a good roommate. He paid rent on time and was overall a drama-free person.

"You know, if God were to grant me one wish, I would agree to become a man of faith like yourself," I said.

"What would that be?" A smile grew on his lips, but he didn't lift his head. He scooped a bowl in his hand and meticulously spread thick tomato sauce across the food pile on his plate. Kamana was a large man. His oval-shaped body stood at about six feet four, or as he would say, one meter and ninety-five.

"I really like this girl," I said, "but I'm stuck! If there's a God, I'd pray to him and ask for an answer." Kamana was one of those people who said that they talked to God, but I doubted his psychic powers, or anyone's.

When I was twelve years old, our house girl and babysitter,

Claud, claimed she had visions of God at night and would tell us stories about what she saw and heard in the morning. Her favorite book in the Bible was Revelations; even the songs she liked were frightening and talked about the end of the world. One night, my younger brother and I sat around the burning charcoal stove while she cooked dinner. I asked her to wake me up the next time she had a night vision so that I might see God myself.

A couple of days later, I received a pat on the shoulder in the middle of the night. I woke up, and Claud was standing tall next to my bed. "Come!" she whispered to me, trying to be careful not to wake up my brother. Staggering out of my bed, I followed her to an open window. She had pulled the curtains in our bathroom. I hesitated for a second. I wasn't sure if I was ready to meet God, an angel, or whatever celestial being Claud was seeing. My heart was pounding.

She held my arm as I climbed atop the bathtub to better glimpse what was happening in the sky. I peered up through the small window, and there was . . . well, nothing! I rubbed my eyes and looked again. There were bright stars in the sky, but they were no brighter than on any other night. It was the same night sky as it had always been, and I didn't see God.

Disappointed, I kept any form of faith or spiritism at arm's length after that night with Claud. I became a skeptic on issues of faith and religion because of it, or so I told myself.

That said, I saw life in two categories: things I could control and things outside my sphere of influence that affected me still. It was the latter group that bothered me. Prayer, through some sort of cosmic order or karmic justice, seemed to be the only medium that could exert influence in this somewhat elusive realm. I was ready to pray to all the gods and be in the good graces of the universe just to be with Karen.

"Is this about Karen?" Kamana had met her when she'd visited me on one occasion.

"Yes, it's about her," I said. "You can't believe it, but I asked her out, and she told me to wait for two years. Can you imagine? It's driving me crazy! I played along at first because I thought she would change her mind if we continued to see each other," I said. "But now she's leaving town."

"It sounds like she pulled a 'Jacob' on you," he said, still chewing food.

"A 'Jacob'?"

"Have you heard of this guy in the Bible called Jacob?" he said. "He had a major crush on this girl, Rachel, and when he asked to marry her, her dad told him to wait for seven years and work for it first."

"For real?"

"Yeah! It gets even more interesting." Kamana laughed. "So, he waited and worked for her father, but after seven years, they gave him a different girl because her older sister was also single and had to get married first, according to tradition."

"No way!" I said. "He got screwed so badly. I'm having a hard time wrapping my head around two years already. Seriously, though, I'm not religious. Yet I prayed on my way home today for Karen and me to work somehow." I poured myself a cup of black tea and extended one to Kamana. "Do you think God will answer my prayer?" I asked Kamana as if he were Peter the Apostle himself. "Two years is a long time to wait for somebody. Well, maybe not for Jacob, but it feels like an eternity to me!"

Kamana paused as he stirred two spoonfuls of sugar into his steaming cup of tea, the spoon hitting the sides, causing a clinking sound.

"I don't know, Saba. You should do things the other way round."

"What do you mean?"

"Build a relationship with God first and make your prayer requests after."

"What does that mean?"

"Have you heard of the phrase 'Seek the Kingdom of God first, and all these things will be given to you'?" Kamana said. "That's how things should happen if you want to embrace the Christian faith."

"Look, I really like her, okay? Why would God be against it?"

"That's not to say that He is. It's more of a process issue," he said. "Let me put it another way. Every man or woman has three needs: physical, emotional, and spiritual. To God, spiritual needs supersede the other two kinds. So, if you come to God, the first thing He makes right is your spiritual life. That's what Christianity is all about, in a nutshell. God taking care of your spiritual needs puts everything else into a better perspective."

"I've never heard it explained like that," I said. "Well, I'd pray to God to see Karen again somehow. I'm heartsick because she's leaving, and I don't know if I will ever see her again after she moves to a different country."

"Bro, if you want to be serious about your faith, prayer should be a lifestyle," he said. "I know that most people remember to pray only when they're in trouble or need something . . ."

"Man, that's a little insensitive! Things start somewhere, you know," I said, a bit aggravated.

"How would you feel about a relationship where someone only calls when they need something from you or have a problem? Well, it's the same thing with God."

"Man, don't worry about it! I'm sure I'll figure it out!" I said. "You never miss a chance to be preachy, do you?"

For a man who prayed before every meal and every night's sleep as Kamana did, prayer was a lifestyle. However, nights like these would give me second thoughts about having him as a roommate. His proselytizing was annoying, especially when I felt vulnerable.

New Business Proposal

o·o·o·o·o·o·o·o·o·o·o·o·o·o·o·o·o·o·o·o·

Albert and I stood next to each other, rehearsing our talking points and double-checking the figure-filled presentation. Dressed above the average person in the room, I was wearing a white shirt tucked into a pair of business pants. I flipped through the fifteen slides to refresh my memory, determined to avoid reading from the screen too much during the presentation.

"AB, are you ready?" I looked at Albert as we completed dividing tasks.

The windows were ajar, and I could feel the morning breeze flowing through the room from the outside. I drank from my coffee mug as we waited for everyone to arrive and sit in the conference room. Mr. Sadiki arrived. The power strip soon ran out of sockets as more people rushed in and took a seat around the space, connecting their laptops to the power outlet. Chairs in the conference room sat far lower than the table. Those who rested their arms on the table looked as if they were holding on to a flotation device. One would have thought that the chairs and tables came from two different carpenters who didn't speak to each other, but they all came from the same vendor. Our office furniture and equipment were cheap—yet another sign of our struggling finances. The computers worked fine, however, except for the batteries, which died after a few months.

"Our proposal to drive revenue and stay competitive rests on three pillars," I started my presentation, facing a curious audience. "Partnerships, branding, and execution."

I introduced the new global business proposal and its potential revenues for about fifteen minutes. Albert took over the second half of the presentation to discuss what the new plan meant for the company's day-to-day operations. He outlined what steps needed to be made to improve business margins.

Group trip planning and commission fees on bookings were our two most significant sources of revenue. Our submitted proposal suggested that the company gradually expand partnerships with hotels, resorts, and travel agencies to countries beyond East Africa. We wanted our company to focus on countries with major natural attractions and a significant flow of tourists to improve our offerings and client base.

"Great job, guys! I liked the presentation," Mr. Sadiki said to our relief after we concluded the thirty-minute talk with two minutes to spare. "I want you to clarify the milestones you mentioned on that previous slide and the related timeline, though."

The projector flickered from a loose connection and an overused power strip.

"Try to include a Gantt chart that shows what needs to happen and when," Mr. Sadiki suggested.

"Will do," I said. "We could start with looking into partnerships in places such as Livingstone and Cape Town."

"I agree!" Mr. Sadiki said. "AB, I want you to go to Zambia and Malawi and see if we can secure partnerships with hotels and travel agents in that region."

"Will do, sir," Albert said.

"Questions?" Mr. Sadiki asked the quiet room. Everyone avoided eye contact with him.

"I think it's clear to me," one colleague called Mario said before a quiet yawn escaped his lips. I couldn't tell if he was sleepy, annoyed, or hungry. He looked as if he hadn't had his breakfast meal yet. People rarely asked questions during Monday morning team meetings, except for Mario. Everyone else kept interactions with the boss to the absolute minimum.

We'd just received the green light on our new business proposal. The following steps were to go on a scouting mission for new partnership opportunities, starting in southern Africa.

I hoped I would be the one to go to Zambia instead of Albert, as Karen had been living there in Livingstone for about six months. She worked for a nonprofit organization focused on helping local women entrepreneurs start and grow their businesses, something she was passionate about. She would always make it a point to share with me the research papers or books on microfinance institutions she was reading. "The Economic Lives of the Poor" by Abhijit Banerjee and Esther Duflo was the most recent one.

I walked out of the meeting with mixed feelings. I was happy my boss liked our presentation. Still, I disliked him calling for my colleague to go to Zambia instead of me. Seeing Karen again this soon on my company's dime would be amazing! Desperate, I knew that the more days we spent apart, the more we would grow apart and lose any connection we had.

My office chair swung back and forth as I leaned back, staring at the branches of the angel trumpet tree protruding from behind my office window. The tree had grown tall enough to be seen from the second floor of our office building.

Its vivid yellow flowers bloomed bright from the morning sun. For a second, I stopped questioning why we had kept this plant and why we let it grow this tall near our office building. Trumpet trees are poisonous, but only to humans. Bees didn't seem to care. They flew into the ripe flowers in groups of three without second thoughts, as if they knew something we didn't.

"Hey, AB!" I said, rubbing my eyes clear after staring outside for a while.

"What's up, Saba!"

"Look, can I be the one to go to Zambia?" I asked sheepishly.

"Hell no!" he replied. "You know the boss asked me to go."

Even before asking, I had known what Albert would say. The chances of anyone, much less AB, ceding an international travel opportunity to me were close to zero. International trips offered a supplemental income in travel stipends, meals, and incidentals. Such trips were a coveted commodity, so much so that they had become a way to entice talent to join MBT. Opportunities to travel for work were almost on a par with health insurance benefits in attracting new recruits, particularly the younger working generation.

Livingstone

o·o·o·o·o·o·o·o·o·o·o·o·o·o·o·o·o·o·o·

I climbed aboard the small propeller plane—my connecting flight at the Kenneth Kaunda airport in Lusaka, Zambia—and took an open window seat. The aircraft is one of the two daily connections to the southern city of Livingstone, where tourists and visitors flock over the weekend.

"We're overbooked," a flight attendant explained to a woman who was the last to climb up the tiny ladder fitted on the plane's door.

"So, what do I do? I can't miss this plane," the woman, who looked to be in her midfifties, asked the flight attendant with her boarding pass in hand.

"Don't worry! You won't miss your connection. I will show you where to sit." The flight attendant helped the woman onto the plane and ushered her into the cockpit next to the two pilots.

"Is it legal to do that?" My eyes beamed at the flight attendant's ability to push the limits of the African adage "There's always room for one more."

"That's a first-class seat," said a Chinese passenger next to me before putting his red passport in his pocket and fastening his seat belt.

As the plane sped down the runway under the high sun, a shadow hurried down my leg, cutting it in half between a shaded area and a lit one. The bright sunlight made my eyes squint as I looked out the window. The engine noises sounded louder than those of a larger commercial airline. I lowered the Hublot's shade as the plane took off, and pulled my phone out of my pocket to check the time. It was 2:24 in the afternoon.

This was a business trip to Zambia. Albert had finally ceded his travel opportunity to me—not of his own volition, however, but because of an unfortunate illness. He had developed a severe case of malaria a week before his trip and had to find a last-minute replacement.

"Are you here for business or pleasure?" I asked the Chinese man.

"I am here for business."

"Same. I work in the tourism industry as a travel agent," I said, without waiting for him to ask me what I was here for.

"My colleagues and I are in mining. We work in the Copperbelt Province." He pointed at two other men sitting behind us. Unlike his colleagues, he was dressed business casual in a fine button-down shirt and glasses. The two men behind us were in baggy T-shirts and had scars on their faces and missing teeth, as if they'd just gotten out of jail. Before I could ask any more questions, he plugged head-phones into his ears and connected them to his phone.

Mining is an old industry in this region and accounts for most export revenues for the Zambian government. The Copperbelt region extends from northern Zambia to neighboring Congo. Since American scout and adventurer Frederick Burnham visited this area in 1895, it has been subjected to foreign investment and mineral exploitation. Word has it he saw natives wearing copper bracelets and got curious about where they came from. The metal's applications have expanded since then, from bracelets to all kinds of electronics, wiring, and plumbing needs that feed an ever-growing global economy. Over the years, financing for the mining industry has shifted from Western capital investments to increasingly Eastern—or more precisely, Chinese—investments.

I turned my head to the right and looked at the view below the plane's oval-shaped window. I slowly laid my head against the plane's wall and closed my eyes.

It was moments like these that I missed having Karen around. If she were here, we would have started a conversation about the mining industry and the impact of foreign investments on the local economy. She was the reason I kept myself informed about current literature on such questions in the first place.

Before she'd moved to Zambia, Karen had often texted me to share articles from her favorite economists such as Esther Duflo, William Easterly, Steven Radelet, and Paul Collier. I enjoyed authors who struck a more pragmatic balance in their works than the critics. I mean, what's the point of telling us everything wrong with our world without offering a solution or a practical course of action to remedy the issues?

An almost indecipherable announcement blasted through the cabin speaker as we descended into Livingstone. I could feel my entrails drop as the captain abruptly changed the plane's altitude. I had planned to land in Livingstone a couple of days early to spare some time to visit the city and meet Karen before the workweek began.

Sunset on the Zambezi

o·o·o·o·o·o·o·o·o·o·o·o·o·o·o·o·o·o·o·o·

The driver from a helicopter company came to pick me up at my hostel early in the morning. I jumped in the car when I saw him and clicked my seat belt in place.

"I want to sit in the front seat of the helicopter during the tour," I said to the driver as soon as the car took off. "What should I do? Do I have to pay extra?" I asked, anxious. I had read from the reviews that the front seats on the helicopter ride had a magnificent view.

"No! Tourists sit according to their weight. I can't guarantee you will get the front seat on the helicopter." He kept his eyes on the road as we drove left on the tarmac. "But we usually prefer couples to take the two front seats."

"For real?" I said. "Well, I have a date, if that's what it takes," I said with gusto, before my tone faded and betrayed my sincerity.

That moment when an innocent comment resurfaces more

profound questions about my life and relationship. Karen was my date for the day, but "couple" was too strong a label, too inexact. But I said just enough to get a better shot at the falls. Besides, it was silly that couples got first dibs on the best seats even though they paid the same price as everybody else.

Karen came running toward me as soon as she arrived at the travel agent's office, where I was waiting for her. She leaped into my arms, and we hugged for about a minute—ten seconds for each month I'd gone without seeing her in my life. She clasped me so tightly that her body sank into mine . . .

"Everyone, come near, come near!" the lead guide yelled and interrupted us. "Good morning, everyone! I'm your lead guide today, and I'll explain what we will do. The helicopter will take you on a loop around the waterfall on both sides of the border. Don't worry, you don't need a visa to fly over Zimbabwe," he laughed.

The waterfall on the Zambezi River divides two countries: Zambia and Zimbabwe. You can visit the waterfall on either side. As with other natural attractions shared by countries, tourists and locals naturally argue about which side of the country has the best view. Karen had only been to the Zambian side on foot and had never seen the waterfalls from above. The helicopter ride would take us around the waterfall and give us a bird's-eye view.

I signaled Karen to walk in front of the group of six tourists, including one couple. The lead guide asked us to stand and wait in a shaded area. The helicopter completed another trip and gently touched down at the center of a massive H painted over the helipad. Wind from the blades' rotation blasted on our faces, sending Karen's curly hair flying. The guide finally gestured to board the helicopter. We approached with our heads tucked into our chests to avoid having the blades chop them off clean.

"You two come sit in front," the guide said, pointing at us.

"Yes!" I inwardly jumped for joy while waiting for Karen to climb on board. Standing outside next to the lead guide, my driver threw me a conspiratorial smile and a thumbs-up as Karen and I took the front seat.

Our visit to Victoria Falls fell on a clear day, and its T-shaped canyon glowed from the ground below. Water levels were highest at this time of the year. The sun's reflection on the upper bed gave the gushing waters a dark silver tone that faded into a lighter color as the river dumped the water with intensity over the earth's crack and down a bottomless pit. The waterfall propelled a cloud of showers into the sky and then back to the ground, earning its local name: Mosi-oa-Tunya, "the Smoke that Thunders." The river's upper bed lay away from the cliff's edge, serene and surrounded by green vegetation. Patches of land interrupted a flat surface of calm waters, which gently drew winding branches from a linear flow upstream.

Next to me, Karen used her iPhone to film the adventure to immortalize the moment. A massive headset covered her ears to insulate them against the rotor's noise.

"This is the best day ever!" Karen said through the tiny microphone fitted on the headset.

"The world's largest waterfall, right before our eyes." I smiled.

It was almost midday when the helicopter ride finished. I made it a point to thank and tip my car driver. I knew he'd had something to do with us getting the front seat.

o · o · o · o · o · o ·

WE DROVE NORTH AND STOPPED near the Zambezi, the river that feeds the waterfall. I pulled my Canon camera out of the bag again as soon as we arrived. I had left the camera bag unzipped the entire time of the helicopter ride. Karen started posing in front of the camera. With the river in the background, I took a few pictures of her.

My fingers browsed through the photographs I had taken one by one, occasionally using the zoom-in button to get a better look at the picture's composition.

The driver was still with us. He was in his convertible three-row jeep, parked a stone's throw away from where we were, listening to the radio.

As I walked back to the car to get snacks, the driver stormed out, wagging his finger in Karen's direction.

"Crocodiles! *Crocodiles!*" he yelled. "Get out! There are crocodiles in the water!"

I turned around, and Karen was sitting down by the riverbank with her legs partially submerged in the river, up to the line where she had rolled up her pant legs. Her hands were also in the water. She was feeling the river as it washed through her fingers.

"Please don't get eaten by crocodiles." I rushed over to her. "Don't get us in trouble!"

Karen, unfazed, nonchalantly stood up. I extended my hand to help her and instinctively wrapped my arms around her. She stroked my back in reciprocation. The thought of losing her to crocodiles or anyone else really terrified me.

"Ew, your hands are wet!"

Karen laughed as she mischievously used my T-shirt as her hand towel.

"I missed that smile, you know." I pressed her against my chest again and kissed her forehead. "Do you want to go sit somewhere? I have snacks. Let's go sit next to the other couple." I pointed at two people who sat nearby.

"'The other couple,' huh?" Karen said, unable to erase the smile off her lips. "So we're a couple now?"

"Well, I'd like us to be. Wouldn't you?"

"I think we already had this conversation."

"That's not fair, Karen. It's hard for me to wait for that long. We don't even live in the same country anymore."

"So, you don't like me anymore?"

"Look at me," I said. "I came all the way to see you. You know the answer to that question."

"Did you come here for me or because your company sent you here?"

"How can you say that?" I said. "Can we just enjoy this moment, please? I don't want to have a fight with you right now."

"Hey, do you guys want to join us?" The couple pulled two beers from their cooler box and invited us to hang out and wait for the sunset with them. We sat by the riverside and drank beer for the rest of the afternoon until the skies turned to gold. The falling night changed the dye of riverside vegetation into a ghostly black and the water into a blend of platinum and gold.

Our driver drove us back to our place after nightfall, dropping off Karen first and me last. When I got to my place that night, it was around 8 p.m., and I immediately went to my room. I was staying at a hostel nicknamed "The Brothel," supposedly branded after its colorful nights. However, the night at the hostel was surprisingly calm, despite its nickname.

I lay on my bed, gazing at the woven ceiling above my bedroom. A mosquito net hung above my head, untied.

The reality of living so far away from Karen was settling in. A long-distance relationship is hard to uphold. How could a long-distance nonrelationship possibly stand? Fate had brought Karen and me together but had somehow failed to provide us with the opportunity to grow closer and build a relationship.

The phone rang beside me, sending vibrations through the bed where I rested. I let it ring twice before I answered.

"This is Kenneth. Sorry for calling you this late. I just wanted to confirm our meeting tomorrow."

"Hi, Kenneth, yes, the meeting is still on. I'm here for a week before heading to Malawi next."

"Sounds good. See you tomorrow, then."

I hung up the phone and threw it on my bed.

Kenneth was one of my company's potential business partners in Zambia. He managed a local tour guide company in both Zambia and neighboring Malawi.

I dreamed of having some sort of brake pedal that could stop the train of life, just so I could figure out my love life, career, and travel aspirations one at a time. However, reality insisted that I do it all simultaneously. Life was always on the move, as if getting too comfortable would suck the life out of our existence. As if discomfort was life itself.

A New Connection

o·o·o·o·o·o·o·o·o·o·o·o·o·o·o·o·o·o·o·

A crowd stood in a herd on a neon-lit balcony outside the bar, cheering on the band. Mint-flavored scents filled the air despite a gentle breeze blowing from the lake nearby. Hookah smoke slightly obstructed the view of musicians and added dramatic effect to the performance. It was jazz night at Cape Maclear hotel.

"Nice tattoo!" I said to a girl who stood next to me. She had the words *love always* inked on her left shoulder in bold italics.

"Thanks!" she said after pausing for a couple seconds to look at the stranger complimenting her. "I'm Isabelle! Call me Izzy!" She passed her Carlsberg beer, locally known as "The Green," to her left hand and extended her hand.

"Do you have any tattoos yourself?" she asked with a smile, releasing my hand.

"I have no body art on me, but I can appreciate it on others," I said. "How long have you been in Malawi?"

"Two years. I live in the capital, but I make the four-hour drive from Lilongwe to this lake at least once every month. Being here by this lake makes me happy."

"Malawi is my second stop after Zambia. I work as a travel agent and I'm scouting for hotel and travel deals in this region. As you know, Cape Maclear is the busiest resort on Lake Malawi."

The bassist sat behind his instrument, plucking at its strings with his head down. The groove drummer was the life of the four-person band. He was dancing with his upper body at the rhythm of his own beat. He wore a big smile and hit the drums and cymbals with enthusiasm and intensity.

"Hey, I'm almost done here. I was going to check out this party if you want to join me?" Izzy said. She looked at me, unafraid to ask a stranger out. Her eyes didn't even blink. She stared at me without hesitation or second thought, as if it were a foregone conclusion that I would follow her if she wanted me to.

"Where is it?"

"It's more like a local party with traditional music," she said. "Come, let's go."

"Sure, why not," I said after clearing my throat. Exhaled puffs of hookahs left an aromatic scent in the air.

Izzy and I left the bar, the sound of the saxophone fading away, and headed down a dark alley leading to the nearby village.

Leaving Karen in Zambia had left me feeling lonely and perplexed. I had always been a solutions person but was running out of options to make things work with her. Waiting for Karen for two years was a colossal sacrifice, particularly when I would meet other women who enjoyed my company.

The dark night had already fallen on the small village as we walked down a back alley, using Izzy's flashlight for visibility. About thirty minutes later, we ran into a crowd congregating at an open-air compound, drinking beer at what looked like a neighborhood block party.

A loudspeaker blasted the local hit "Nilibe Problem," which means "I don't have a problem" in the local language. People loosely danced to the music, boxes of Chibuku in hand.

Chibuku, the local brew, comes in a one-liter carton and tastes like a mixture of vodka and oatmeal. It's cheap, filling, and more enjoyable for the locals than the more expensive "Green."

"Two Greens, please!" I ordered a couple of Carlsberg beers from the bartender at the event. A flickering lightbulb hanging over the bar counter cast barely enough light for the bartender to count his cash.

"This is unlike anything I've seen," I said to Izzy. "How did you know about this event?"

"There are a lot of things you don't know about me." She shook her head, amused. "You haven't seen nothing yet!"

"Okay! What else should I know about you?"

Izzy's ear jewelry glowed in the dark. An assortment of helix earrings lined her ear, filling all the space you could pierce.

Three men in unusual costumes hit the dirt stage about an hour after we arrived. At that point, the loudspeakers playing contemporary music went dead silent. Tribal drums, the eerie sounds of ankle bells, and cheers from the crowd set the rhythm for the dancers instead.

The tribal dancers wore wooden masks painted pitch-black. Pink eyes stared and hung above an expressionless wooden mouth. The masks looked like they would fall off their faces at any minute.

The dancers stripped off several layers of shabby clothes to reveal that hay and banana leaves covered their invisible body frames. They strode around like a moving bush and shook their hips to the rhythm of a fast drumbeat. Their legs swung side to side in frenetic motions that shoved dirt into the air, and the audience applauded and released loud screams. Seemingly in a trance, a hysterical crowd rained money on the performers.

"This is Gule Wamkulu—'The Great Dance,'" Izzy explained.

The excitement in the crowd was palpable and intense, as if the dance were something more than casual entertainment, something occult or transcendental.

"What's 'The Great Dance'?"

"It's a spiritual dance that is part of a cult, long practiced by people of this region. The performers are from a secret society called the Nyau."

"How on earth do you know these things? You're not even from this country—or are you an anthropologist?"

"My grandparents came from Armenia. I'm Ethiopian of Armenian descent. As an engineer, I've been spending a lot of time with tribal leaders in my consulting work for a water and sanitation nonprofit. We work with local communities on prevention and risk assessment measures against flooding problems," she said. "Speaking of flooding, can you get me another beer, please?"

"Sure!" I replied. "Another Carlsberg?"

"No! Let's try the Chibuku and loosen up a little."

The Lake of Stars

o·o·o·o·o·o·o·o·o·o·o·o·o·o·o·o·o·o·o·o·

It was a Thursday morning. I took a stroll on the beach early to catch the deep orange sunrise over Lake Malawi. My head was still buzzing from the previous night. A puppy trotted along the coast near me, wagging his tail and hoping to catch leftovers from the fishers' bounty. A few people were washing dishes in the small splashing waves. Some were bathing, and others collected cooking water into jerricans. A hustling, poor village where beauty and misery existed side by side.

I sat on a rock a few meters away, observing the commotion of busy fishers and local villagers. The sun painted the sky with a blend of yellow and orange. Whistling in from the lake, a cool wind stroked my face and lifted open my heavy eyelids.

It wasn't until around eight in the morning that I met Izzy at the reception of our lodge. After eating a protein-filled breakfast—an omelet, sausages, beans, a piece of tomato, and bread—we left the beachfront lodge.

We trekked the dusty laterite road flanked by trees and bushes. Izzy had the hiking trail map we had collected at the reception. Despite my job, my sense of direction has always been subpar. This one skill, or lack thereof, had tormented me when I'd considered changing careers to join the travel industry, almost as much as my family's objections had.

"Do you know where we're going?" I said. We had been walking for an hour, but Izzy had yet to open the map we'd bought for directions. She just led the way, making left turns and right turns without hesitation.

"I've been here before," she said. "I regularly come to this place."

"Is that how you found out about the party last night?"

"Yeah! I get invited to these things," she said. "I worked with this community for a while, and I maintained connections with faith leaders from my previous job."

"What did you do for work before?"

"Women issues. Mostly at the intersection of faith and culture."

"The dance last night looked like a cultlike ritual, for sure," I said. "It was wild."

"Yep! This place has entertained many rituals for a long time: local rituals, Christian rituals . . ."

"Christian rituals?"

"Yeah! Have you heard of the Livingstonia Mission?"

"I have not."

"It's a bunch of Scottish missionaries who wanted to establish a Christian mission site here at the end of the nineteenth century. Malaria and mosquitoes drove them out, though," Izzy said, wagging the water bottle she had at the surrounding hills.

"How do you know these things?" I laughed. "I thought you were a civil engineer."

Trees scattered around the field stretched before us. Mammoth baobabs lined the path, their size imposing. They stood majestic and naked on a short, yellowish grass carpet burned by constant exposure to sunlight, typical of savanna-style vegetation.

We sat in a shaded area to take a break and hydrate underneath one of the trees. The baobab was so gigantic, you could carve a two-bedroom house from its trunk alone. A giant birthed by Mother Earth as if to give us perspective and remind us how small and fragile we are. How powerless we are against the forces of nature, how insignificant and futile our worries and quarrels. The clouding shadow of the baobab tree made us feel as small as the ants running on the ground beneath our feet.

"Before I came to Malawi, I worked with a nonprofit in North and Central Africa promoting women's rights. I wanted to do something meaningful with my life, you know. A job that makes me feel like I'm making a difference."

Red Martian dust covered the stone we sat on and printed a patch on Izzy's blue pants. My gray shorts concealed dust better.

"I think there comes a time where we look for a job like that. I left my old job after it became uninspiring."

"Well, my old job was unhealthy. I mean, dangerous," she said. "I worked on an anti-FGM campaign in the middle of nowhere. Do you know what FGM is?"

"Female genital mutilation?"

"Exactly! I used to work with tribal leaders on these issues and ways to fight the practice in their communities. Do people practice FGM in your culture too?" she said. "It's such a health risk and just plain wrong. My former boss didn't set our organization up to address the issue effectively."

The tone of her voice was charged with heavy emotions, which she was trying hard to bottle up, to hide behind her sunglasses and a straw sun hat she was wearing.

The weight of her painful experiences was apparent in the wrinkles drawn on the side of her eyes.

"You can't communicate effectively with someone about changing a cultural issue without taking the time to understand his beliefs. Understand the underlying values before questioning FGM as a religious or cultural imperative," she said. "It's a shame that the average development professional's knowledge of faith and culture doesn't rise beyond popular opinion, in my experience. I advised my boss to train our technical staff on tribal rituals and worldviews of communities practicing FGM, but he thought it unnecessary. Like a broken record, all our strategy and communication pointed to health risks and benefits."

"Interesting! I think most people understand that faith influences behavior..."

"Look, Saba! I've always believed in the idea of an 'ultimate desire,' which is different for different people. This is where people draw the last line, the proverbial hill to die on, if you will. If someone's ultimate desire is some sort of moral or spiritual ideal, pointing to health benefits may not help much. Particularly when said health benefits go against their moral ideal because, for them, this 'ultimate desire' is, by definition, the thing to die for."

"That's an interesting viewpoint, Izzy. Well, people don't do what they do for health benefits alone. Actual or perceived moral duty or public good can be the key factor, as you say."

"That's right. Otherwise, why would a soldier go to war to defend his country, or a firefighter risk his life to pull someone from a burning building? They do it for a greater good, real or perceived."

Nature isolated us from the world, but not in a way that made us feel lonely. Instead, we grew closer as we talked and sat silently between conversations reflecting upon life.

"What's Rwandan culture like?" Izzy asked again. "Do you have a culture that inhibits female sexuality?"

"No! I don't think so!" I said. "Quite the contrary." I laughed.

"Yeah? Tell me about it."

"Traditional Rwandan culture is very different. It's pro-women in that aspect and in many others. In fact, a man's ability to provide the ultimate pleasure to his woman defines his masculinity, if you know what I mean."

"I like that culture." Izzy smiled. Her face beamed with happiness again.

"No kidding! Men get nervous if they can't perform and make it happen, and then they must talk to old people for tips."

Izzy took a sip from her water bottle to hydrate, then handed me the bottle so I could drink. Her voice had become dry from our long conversation and dry weather.

"Should we get going?" Izzy checked the map before we continued walking toward the lake. Our lodge was on the shore of Lake Malawi. We arrived at the water's edge and walked back to our place up the shoreline.

Baobabs followed us like signposts along the dirt walkway with their massive trunk base and shrinking branches that looked like T. rex arms.

Visibly tired and drawing curious looks from village kids, we made our way along the lakeshore, where a few fishermen washed their nets.

"Is there a simple way back to our lodge from here?" Izzy said.

"This path isn't clear for someone to walk through, for sure." We had just discovered that part of the shoreline was full of trees and rocks.

"Let's ask the fishermen to take us back to our lodge, then. I'm too tired to make another four-and-a-half-hour walk," Izzy said.

"It looks like they're having some downtime," I replied. A few fishermen sat on their dugout canoes, chatting.

One fisherman was repairing his net with a wooden netting needle. He sat in the sand with his toes sticking out of holes in a fishing net spread across his lap and extended legs.

I talked to the fisherman to ensure he had a motorized fishing boat before giving him three thousand kwachas, about four US dollars, for the ride. I put the pink stash of money in his hand, in a stack of hundred-kwacha bills, and we made a deal for him to take us back to our lodge.

Izzy and I promptly got into the boat alongside the fisherman, named Nestor. Two of his kids, ten and twelve years old, also jumped into the boat.

"They don't have school today," Nestor assured us before we could ask any parenting-related questions.

Nestor had hooked an outboard motor to his rusty rowboat. We drifted away from the lakeshore, drawing a trail in the water as we sailed onward to the background noise of the loud motor.

About a few minutes later, the motor crackled and coughed. It coughed a couple more times and then went completely silent.

Nestor stood up and yanked the pull string to get it going again, but without success. He tried a few times, to no avail . . .

"Everything is fine," Nestor said with a thick local accent.

"My mom taught me how to swim," Izzy said. She sat tranquil with her shades and straw hat on, leaning on a rear crossbeam.

Nestor kept trying to start the motor without success as I watched in disbelief. His two kids, seemingly unfazed by the whole situation, started diligently scooping water out of the boat into the lake. They looked like they had done this before.

"Everything is fine!" Nestor said again.

I stared at Nestor, my eyes wide open as if to say, *Stop saying that! We have a broken motor and a leaky boat! How can you say everything is okay?*

Even though I'd grown up near a lake like this one, I'd never learned to swim correctly. So, my life was in the hands of Nestor's preteen sons and their ability to bail us out faster than the water was coming in through the boat's floor.

After his futile attempt at restarting the engine, Nestor took off his sleeveless shirt and waved at his friends on the lakeshore.

Like an act of divine providence, one of his friends, whom we could barely see from a distance, noticed something was amiss. He immediately sent a mechanic in a small one-person rowboat.

We sat in the boat for about fifteen minutes as we waited for our help to arrive. The mechanic finally got on board and immediately fixed the engine.

Thirty minutes later, we safely docked near our lodge. I left the boat first and Izzy followed me. We graciously thanked the entire crew, particularly the two kids, who were now our heroes.

Izzy and I grabbed a couple beers each and sat on the front porch of our hotel lodge as the yellow sun sank over the horizon. We laughed about our adventure and talked about the majestic baobabs adorning the roads we had hiked on earlier. We laughed about Nestor and his two kids, who had skipped school to work on their dad's boat. About how our simple ride back had taken an unpredictable turn and almost left us stranded in the middle of Lake Malawi—the Lake of Stars.

Explorer David Livingstone came up with the nickname "the Lake of Stars" after observing bright specks of light hovering over the waters at night. However, the lights he saw weren't from celestial objects or stars in the sky, as he initially thought. They were from fishermen like Nestor who carried lamps in their canoes at night while fishing.

Izzy sat beside me, rocking back and forth in a swing chair.

"I had a great time today, Saba," she said before emptying her Carlsberg beer bottle into her mouth. "Thanks for hanging out with me!" she added in a gentle voice.

"Same!" I said pensively.

The night was calm except for the sounds of crickets chirping around us, the occasional frog croaking nearby but never to be seen.

"So, what do you want to do now?" Izzy looked at me nonchalantly, her hair down. "It's getting cold outside. I think I'll just go to my room now . . . want to join me?"

I silently gazed into her eyes.

"Well, I'd like to . . . but I must prepare for a meeting tomorrow. Maybe next time," I sighed.

"All right, good night, Saba," she said, visibly disappointed.

I returned to my room alone and immediately locked the door behind me.

"Argh!" I buried my head under the pillowcase and screamed for a good minute.

My connection with Izzy was effortless and natural. But strangely enough, hooking up with her now felt like cheating on Karen, even as the only commitment I had from Karen was to "wait and see."

After I regained my composure, I sat on my bed, caressing my clean-shaven chin, thinking about what I should do. I leaped from the bed, frantically reached out to my phone in my pocket, and started typing on the bright screen: *Hey, Karen, it was great to see you again last weekend. Just wanted to say I like you . . . and you won! I will wait for you. Counting down the months now, bye!*

CHAPTER 4

Layover in Paris

o·o·o·o·o·o·o·o·o·o·o·o·o·o·o·o·o·o·o·o·

A blue sky stretched ahead as the midday sun enhanced the shades of greenery. Colorful houses lined the canals integrated into the city structure like a puzzle. I stood on the platform, waiting for my train connection to arrive. I closed my eyes and then opened them again to heal my drifting focus, without success. A synthesized and robotic voice shouted a long announcement in Dutch, which seemed to take forever to complete. At that point, I had given up trying to understand spoken Dutch after telling the ticket operator that I needed to buy a train instead of a train ticket! "Het kost u veel geld—'it's going to cost you a lot of money,'" he'd joked.

Working in the service industry, I imagined locals would appreciate the effort tourists made to learn their language. The cultural gesture was worth the inevitable embarrassment. I even bought a debit card to blend in with modern life, and instead of traveling with an entire stash of dollar bills, I went with half a stash. I split my travel budget money in half, put one half on a prepaid debit card, and kept the other half in cash, just in case. Perhaps the most exciting part was that my mom drove me to the airport on my business trip and convinced a few cousins and relatives to accompany me to the airport. Like a wedding convoy, we followed each other on my way to the airport and spent time together until I checked in. Those relatives who didn't come called and wished me a safe trip.

I glanced around to double-check the numbered platform signs hung beneath a maze of power supply lines as the train whooshed by the platform.

At last, an automated voice spoke in English and confirmed that the gate to the Thalys train to Paris-Nord was on Platform 14A. "The first-class tickets are at the front of the train," the voice announced. I had purchased the cheapest ticket available. Paying extra for first-class or premium economy didn't make financial sense to me. We all get there at the same time, after all. My budget was tight, and things were much more expensive in Amsterdam than in my home country. This was a detour I'd planned from my business trip, and any expenses relating to it were out-of-pocket.

I boarded the train last and dropped my backpack on the floor as soon as I made it inside. My puffy winter jacket gave the seat extra padding. I had booked one of the two fold-down seats at the back of a train car, near where people board the train. This was my first time experiencing weather below 10 degrees Celsius. My body was as confused as my bearings—the sun was out, but it was cold outside.

The locals didn't seem to care, however. They pedaled their bicycles in all directions in the city streets and hauled their groceries in front-mount carriages. Earlier that day, I had walked around

Amsterdam city center to drop off my enormous suitcase at a public storage facility.

Opposite my seat was a woman wearing a pink sweater under her winter coat. She sat clamping tightly to her handbag as if bracing for some impact, hugging it as she would a loved one when in need of reassurance. Her hunched posture made it look as if she were carrying too much baggage and sinking under a lot of weight. But the only thing that hung from her neck was a small digital camera and her long, dark textured hair. Her eyes stared out the window pensively, her aura serene against the backdrop of the fast-changing world beyond the train window. Like a perfect life metaphor, our little cabin was a safe shelter against the hazards of a fast-paced life, a momentary pause against the inevitable grind for survival and self-actualization.

Our eyes met when she turned her gaze back inside. We timidly broke eye contact. I hadn't realized I was staring at her the whole time.

"Are you going to Paris too?" I said, as if being on a direct train to Paris wasn't obvious enough to tell where she was going.

"Yes." She looked at me more comfortably this time. "It's my first time. I'm Abby!"

"Saba! Nice to meet you."

A couple of other passengers sat in the front seats of the train car, slumped in their cushy red velvet seats. One of them, a bald man in glasses, struggled to read his stack of papers. The daily newspapers spread out past his seat as if they had exploded from an overpacked suitcase.

Another passenger stood up and squeezed past our area to check on his bags. He spent a minute going through things in his suitcase and returned to his seat, closing the sliding door between the car's front section and the back area behind him which, in addition to having the cheapest seats, doubled as a space to store extra luggage. It was then just Abby and me, and the sight of streets and buildings flashing past the train window.

"Where are you from, Abby?" My cultural sensitivity kicked in, not wanting to guess by her looks and accent.

"From Beijing, China."

"Asia is one continent I haven't been to yet. Hopefully, I'll get to visit one day."

The outside world sped by as I leaned back further in my seat and enjoyed the smooth rolling motion of the train.

"You should visit Beijing. The city is a brilliant mix of modern and traditional China," she said. "And we have amazing food!"

"That's my hope, one day. I've been working in the service industry for about one and a half years, and my company is thinking about expanding to the East."

"It's my dream to work in the service industry too," she said in a bubbly tone, rubbing her hands together like a kid on a Christmas morning.

I smiled, surprised by her sudden jovial demeanor. Apprehensive, she leaned back and sat composed in her seat again, like a comedian who had just broken character to show her true heart.

"I just quit my job, and here I am, traveling to Paris." Her eyes lit up, but then she quickly erased her smile again, realizing she was talking to a stranger. Her inquisitive eyes tried to decipher my reaction. I guessed that she was trying to find out whether I was that all-knowing adult she had been dreading all her life who would tell her for the seventy-seventh time, "You do not quit your job unless you have a new one."

"You seem so happy about it," I said with a warm voice.

"I am," she said. "Everyone in my family works the same job until they retire. My parents worked for the government their whole lives, like my grandparents before them. My relatives have been working in the same position as well. I just couldn't do it," she sighed. "Government work pays well back home. They have excellent benefits and everything. It's just not for me, so I had to get out."

"I know what you mean."

"Some people enjoy a sedentary life, go to the same school as their parents, and work the same job until they retire. But such a linear path of life wasn't for me," she continued. "I don't know about you, but people who grow restless when settling in one place can't stand a monotonous and predictable life."

Abby was from a big country, but even that felt too small for her. Her enthusiasm reminded me of the day I'd quit my job to become a travel agent. Our English accents were different. She spoke with pauses between words, and I still had my African intonation despite my attempt at imitating *Voice of America* newscasters over the years. But, for all our differences, we understood each other perfectly. At heart, she and I were the same type of person. We embraced uncertainty with a sense of wonder and rode through life as one would a bicycle—they have to keep moving lest they stop and fall. To such people, comfort is uncomfortable.

"I get you, Abby," I said again. "Let me ask you this—what would you like to do in a perfect world? What would it be if you could have any job you want?"

"I'd open a bakery shop," she said without hesitation. "That's what I want to do. That's why I left China to go to Paris. They have the best culinary schools here. Once I have my degree, I will open a bakery shop—that's what I want."

"That's great, Abby. I'm sure you'll figure it out. It looks like you and I have a few things in common besides buying the cheapest seats on this train."

After arriving in Paris, I wished Abby good luck and took the metro from Gare du Nord to Colonel Fabien station. I marched the rest of the way to my hostel, where I stayed that night.

o · o · o · o · o · o ·

MY FIRST STOP IN PARIS was not the Louvre Museum. It was not the Eiffel Tower either, even though the Iron Lady stood above every house and monument, elevated above Haussmannian buildings in the city. I didn't visit the Moulin Rouge or the cabarets of Montmartre, not until the following day. Instead, my first stop in Paris was an old low-key residential house in the 16th Arrondissement.

I took the metro near my hostel to La Muette station early in the morning. My curiosity grew stronger when I arrived at the gate. Tucked in a peaceful corner of Paris in the Passy neighborhood, the house belonged to a famed French novelist of the nineteenth century named Honoré de Balzac.

An arched sapphire gate stood tall before me and hid the residence from prying eyes, like a scene from Balzac's own short story "La Grande Bretèche." In this short story, Horace Bianchon, the main character, tries to unmask the mystery behind an abandoned manor.

Balzac lived in anonymity under a false name because he owed money to his creditors. Despite his poor financial skills, however, he was a literary genius.

His house had discreet colors: a gray-and-light-green combination. Shutters on the large windows matched the emerald shade of his lawn. A few chairs were scattered outside, as if they were serving a small book club discussion.

Balzac lived here around 1840. His old desk, where he wrote *La Comédie Humaine*, is among the few original pieces of furniture left in his house, which had been turned into a museum.

His own writings covered the wall in white font. A few busts of Balzac created by other artists were also in the exhibition. Cast in stone, his face had a pointed nose and a large mustache that hid his baby cheeks.

I wondered what his life looked like during his time and if he thought he would be as famous as he became several decades after his death. His parents also wanted him to be someone else and do other things for his career. They wanted him to be a clerk, but he refused and chose a different path.

I walked through the house surrounded by framed drawings and sketches, which hung on the wall in pairs, and got to the Red Room, a red-curtained scarlet room with wooden floors. There sat a small table where the famous writer wrote his books. A couple of his manuscripts were at his table, laminated behind a protective film and full of edits, crossed-out words, and notes written in the margins of a printed text.

In the exhibit was his cause of death: a peculiarly ornate white ceramic coffeepot that bears his initials. It sat behind a glass frame and looked deceivingly innocent and harmless. Balzac was a coffee addict. Some say he consumed about fifty cups of coffee daily, which led to his demise.

After visiting the Musée Balzac, I walked around the city until the evening came; then I returned to my hostel. I sat on the fenced rooftop of the hostel overlooking the Sacré-Coeur Basilica. The sky was clear.

Many young people from all over Europe stayed at this hostel, traveling the world on a budget. The cheap bunk beds were a coveted commodity for people whose age was too young or budget too small to afford a decent Parisian hotel. They traveled light, unencumbered by family obligations or the perils of smoking a pack of cigarettes in one evening.

I leaned my back against the fence, looking at the illuminated basilica and Montmartre. My childhood dream had been to go to Paris.

I'd developed a liking for adventure early in life. Besides weekend trips to Lake Tanganyika with my parents, my sister, and my two brothers, my best childhood memories were of watching adventure movies and cartoons.

Around the World in Eighty Days was my favorite cartoon on TV. Based on a novel by Jules Verne, the show tells the story of Phileas Fogg, an English gentleman traveling the world in eighty days, accompanied by his butler, Passepartout, and little Tico. As a kid, I would also stare at planes in the sky and wonder where they were going and what was on the other side of the horizon. I knew it was only a matter of time before I could travel the world myself to find out. Traveling was my way of connecting with others, admiring the beauty of life, and discovering the divine in the intersection of nature and culture.

Although new to me, Paris somehow felt familiar because of her cultural and literary influence. Something about Paris intrigued me, like that first impression you get when discovering a new culture, a new home, a new love, before exciting things become commonplace. The beauty of the details that only the first look provides. That first look documents things that even locals do not see; or maybe they are too accustomed to seeing them, making them invisible.

Rideau Centre

o·o·o·o·o·o·o·o·o·o·o·o·o·o·o·o·o·o·o·o·

A constant stream of pedestrians flowed outside the window wall, carefully waiting for the Walk sign to display before crossing the road. Everyone outside wore furry winter coats and boots. Everyone except for the homeless guy—he sat leaning against a traffic light pole with his legs tucked in a sleeping bag as people hurried past his coin cup.

A patch of snow was sandwiched between the road and the sidewalk where footsteps had melted the ice. Red-and-white buses slowly drove by with sticker ads all over them. Take the Plunge!, one of them read in bold letters.

"Are you Saba?" A six-foot man in skinny blue jeans stood beside me.

"Yeah, that's me!" I said. "Chris, right? Nice to meet you!" I extended a hand to be shaken and pulled back the seat next to me. He put his overcoat on the chair's backrest and took a seat.

Chris worked with *Canadian Traveller* magazine. Mr. Sadiki had put us in contact as MBT explored partnership opportunities in North America, the largest consumer market in the world. We wanted the publication to feature our company for publicity exposure.

"I hear you're interested in the Canadian market?"

"Definitely! We'd like to see more business and Africa-bound trips."

"I like that!" Chris replied. He wore a friendly smile like a professional salesperson.

The sound of elevator music, mixed with chatter in French and Arabic, played in the background alongside the gurgling and crackling of the coffee roasting machine the barista was operating. Bags of coffee beans lined the shelf below the machine, each with a tag displaying its exotic origin.

"Well, we're looking for featured destinations for next year, so great timing! Let me talk to my boss and circle back with detailed price quotations."

The number of repeat and new customers had increased over time at MBT, a credit to the business strategy that Albert and I had put together. Revenues were up by eighteen percent, and the morale was strong at the company. We had secured more partnerships, and the company's visibility was increasing through referrals from existing customers and our advertising and marketing push.

Albert and I had divided regions, each focusing on a distinct part of the world. He oversaw all Africa- and Europe-based partnerships. My job had grown to oversee operations across the Atlantic in North America and Southeast Asia. This strategy allowed us to be more efficient. It prevented the otherwise inevitable fights over who got to travel to which country.

"Is this your first visit to Canada?" Chris sipped coffee in a Bridgehead cup.

"It's my first time here, yes. Any suggestions of what I should do? I'm trying to take in as much as possible."

"Well, during this time, most people go skating on the canal."

"The water canal?" I said louder, raising my voice above the brouhaha in the background.

"Yes, the Rideau Canal," he said. "Winter weather in Ottawa is so reliably cold that it freezes the canal's water solid for people to walk and skate on."

"I've never learned how to skate on ice. But that sounds fun," I said. "I will also visit Montreal before leaving Canada. I'm supposed to meet a friend there." I tilted my ceramic mug to peek inside, pretending to be unsure if I had left any coffee inside.

"Excuse me for a sec," Chris interrupted as he stepped into the restroom.

I picked up my phone to type a few notes from the conversation and check my SMS app for new messages. A knitted winter scarf wrapped around my neck to my chin and mouth. I kept it on despite being in a heated room.

When I scrolled through my messages, I found Karen's texts. The logs of our conversations were endless. A couple sad-face emoji were posted underneath texts where Karen had discussed her relationship with an ex-boyfriend. She wrote about how noncommittal he had been to their relationship and how hard it had been for her to move on, and I hated it. I hated when Karen would talk about being with other men.

About a year had passed since I'd last seen her in Zambia on my business trip. She was currently on vacation, visiting a friend in New York City. As we weren't that far from each other, we'd agreed to commute and meet in the middle—in Montreal.

In the middle was where Karen met me in our yet-to-be-determined relationship. Despite living apart for about a year, I still felt close to Karen. She made a point to be in touch over email or text messages. This constant communication kept alive my hopes of us being together one day. My heart was in a good place at this point. In the beginning, I'd agonized between moving on or waiting for Karen. Eventually, that had settled. Only one path had to prevail. A decision had to be made. So, I'd rolled the dice and resolved to wait and see what happened.

Chris returned from the restroom and sat down. "My girlfriend and I are driving from Ottawa to Quebec City tomorrow. Happy to give you a ride if you haven't bought a bus ticket yet."

We exchanged business cards and chatted a bit more before I left to catch the bus back to my cousin's house, where I was staying.

o · o · o · o · o · o ·

THE DINING TABLE WAS GLOWING. Candles stood in the middle of serving dishes, food bowls, and a bottle of red port wine, which sat two-thirds empty on the dinner table. A Christmas tree lit up one corner of the living room next to a staircase to the second floor from which were strung stockings, little reindeer, red balls, and lightbulbs.

"How was your meeting today, Saba?" my cousin Seth inquired.

I had left the house earlier in the morning to go to Rideau Centre in downtown Ottawa. Seth had been up early as well. He'd gotten up in the morning before his wife and kid to clean the house and plow the snow in his parking lot. We'd caught up then and discussed my itinerary and travel plans before I'd left for my business meeting.

"It went great! I ended up getting a ride to Montreal. So that will save you the trip to the bus station tomorrow," I said. Holiday music played through the TV set and out of surround speakers in the room.

Seth sat at the table along with his wife, Libby, and his brother, Kenny, my other cousin on my mother's side. The dinner table was bright under the light of candles reflecting off the glittering crystals of the chandelier above it.

Mico, Seth and Libby's three-year-old, was sitting on Libby's lap, chewing cut carrots with his baby teeth and holding his fire truck toy in his other hand, reluctant to put down either.

"Baby Mico loves trucks and fire engines, so that's what we got him for Christmas," Seth said before casually planting a kiss on his wife's willing lips.

"Baby Mico, you want to be a firefighter, huh?" Libby talked to her child as she fed him.

Stocked with roast chicken, potatoes, vegetables, goat cheese salad, and gingerbread cookies, the table smelled delicious.

"Saba, so glad you get to visit, man," Seth said. "The last time we saw each other in person was several years ago when we were living in Bujumbura."

"I know. We were babies," I said. "Look at you now!" I turned to the others. "Seth was a smart, chubby kid, the only one who spoke decent English. I remember one time during a family reunion, we played karaoke, and I made up the words of my favorite song, and he corrected my gibberish English." I smiled.

"Yeah, there's this song you would sing all the time, and I'd be like, what on earth are you talking about?"

"Milli Vanilli's 'Girl, I'm Gonna Miss You'!" I laughed.

"That's right!"

"I would just say random words to the verse part, then land on 'Girl, I am gonna miss you.' The only words I could sing right."

"Cheers to reuniting with family and to a prosperous new year ahead." My cousin raised a glass. "And to my beautiful wife and kid, who make my life complete." He winked at Libby.

"Big toast to that," I said. "So thankful for the past year as well. Changing careers was difficult, but I'm glad it's worked out so far and allowed me to come to see you guys after such a long time." My hand carefully raised the full glass again so as not to spill the red wine.

"Well, I'm thankful for you all and for Seth, my husband. We dated for seven years before we got married, and he's still as passionate about us as he was when we first met," Libby said.

"Thank you, love!" Seth kissed his wife.

"To my family!" Kenny raised his beer bottle.

After dinner, I retreated to the guest room and slept on the foldout bed they had arranged for my visit. Marriage had changed my cousin a lot. He was not the turbulent kid he used to be when I'd last seen him. He had become a man with a heightened sense of responsibility.

Electric plugs in his house were all child-proofed, doorknobs had safety covers, and the hot water in the bathroom had a maximum temperature.

For the first time, I could picture myself trading my nomadic, free-roaming life for family life. Maybe I'd settle down in the suburbs of a midsize city somewhere with a wife and a kid and give up always being on the move and traveling worldwide. Would I feel bored? I don't know. Seth seemed happy as a married man. He had leaned into it.

Single life wasn't bad, but I was hitting an inflection point in a life of constant traveling and meeting new people. Maybe it was time for me to turn the page—to stay in one place, start my family, and come home to someone.

However, I was uncertain if this newfound love for sedentary family life was just a result of me spending time with Seth and his family over the holiday season. After all, we emulate the conditions of people we're around despite our highly held notion of independence and free determination.

I didn't know if Karen, the only woman I could see myself settling down with, felt the same way. I would find out soon whether asking her to plant roots somewhere would be the best way to break her self-imposed dating hiatus.

The Iced Car

o·o·o·o·o·o·o·o·o·o·o·o·o·o·o·o·o·o·o·

Snowflakes tenderly parachuted from the sky outside the slightly fogged-up car window. A white expanse of snow ran through adjacent fields, punctuated by the occasional gray, frozen river streams. Like the backdrop of a horror movie, leafless and darkened trees stood tall side by side. Snow trucks and cars skated through Highway 30 ahead of us, ominously flashing red hazard lights.

I rubbed my burning earlobes underneath the thick cotton layer of my winter hat. My ears and fingertips felt as if someone had stuck needles into them, slowly numbing them. Cold weather sneaked into the car like a ghost and tormented my body despite the rolled-up windows. I sat bundled with five layers of clothes on me like corn husks. The backseat vent didn't work, I belatedly learned. The heating in Chris's old Jeep barely provided enough warmth to keep my bones from freezing.

As soon as we drove into Quebec, the familiar sight of Stop signs gave way to more French-friendly Arrêt signs. They stood planted at every intersection, reminding every traveler that people speak a language that's not English here. Alongside road signs in French, the license plates read Je Me Souviens, meaning "I remember" in French.

"What is it they remember?" I said.

"Their defeat by the British!" Chris's girlfriend, who was in the front seat, responded with a famous characterization of the Quebec motto's meaning, which more broadly and officially means "remembering Quebec's history and cultural heritage."

I shivered in the back seat with my arms crossed around my body, counting on my imagination to keep me warm. The thought of meeting Karen again somehow raised my body temperature. I had learned to keep my feelings in check over time, but the prospect of meeting her in Montreal had brought them back like an ocean wave. Heartsick, I raised my freezing bare hands closer to my face from my pocket to check on them. They shook.

Over time, I had come to accept that I cared a lot about Karen. So much so that I would wait for her for a couple of years without seeing other women. Maybe I had bought into the sunk-cost fallacy. I had invested so much time and energy. I had passed up on so many other potential relationships that I was unprepared to count it all as a loss. So, I leaned in, persisted, and resisted the constant urge to go out with other people. In an ironic turn of events, more girls seemed to notice me after I decided I was unavailable!

My heart was at peace with it, however. Karen had stolen it. I feared I might not ever feel the same about any other girl. That said, having the emotional space offered by Karen's dating hiatus allowed me to focus more on my job.

Chris and his girlfriend chatted in the front seats. They were in some sort of argument, unencumbered by a listening stranger in their back seat. She wanted him to move to Quebec City, to move in with her, but he was hesitant because of his job in Ottawa. To her, that was tantamount to a lack of commitment; she was mad at him for it. Uninterested in adding more drama to my life, I reclined in the back seat a little more and tried to doze off.

We crossed the Île aux Tourtes Bridge into Montreal after two and a half hours of driving. My eyes opened in time to see a massive green road sign with white font welcoming us to a multilane bridge to the island of Montreal.

A French enclave in a "dangerously" Anglo-Saxon neighborhood, Quebec is sandwiched between the English-speaking part of Canada and the United States. For this reason, and many more, Quebecois are adamant about preserving their distinct cultural and linguistic identity.

Considering that the French territory stretched from Montreal to Mobile, Alabama, you realize how much land the French lost to their British and American foes in history. The remnants of Anglo-French wars of the distant past, and the rivalry between the former colonial powers, seemed to have left a mark on contemporary Quebec society, inciting a North American version of the Fashoda syndrome, a tendency within French foreign policy in Africa to prioritize asserting French influence in areas susceptible to British influence.

That said, Montreal's spirit is that of "le vivre ensemble," "a shared life," if you will. As we drove, I realized the cultural vibe of Montreal was unlike anything I'd ever seen: Her walls were tall and covered in colorful graffiti. Her people were cosmopolitan and covered in tattoos. They proudly flashed their ink on the edges of their winter garments.

We drove toward the Old Port of Montreal, then continued south toward the city hall, where French President Charles de Gaulle made his controversial "long live free Quebec" speech. He fanned secession flames in the province after arriving in the city through the historic Chemin du Roy road built along the St. Lawrence River in 1737.

The Hôtel de Ville, as the locals call it, stood prominently. The balcony where de Gaulle addressed the people and the open public square looked just as it had in the documentary movie I had seen, except for the crowd. Now only a few people strolled by the snow-covered area, taking pictures.

After about three hours of driving total, Chris pulled into my hotel's parking lot. I thanked him and his girlfriend for the ride and jumped out of the car, desperate to get inside. I walked toward the entrance door, carefully planting one foot after the other to avoid slipping on black ice. The white of the snow on the roadside had deteriorated into a dark gray where car tires had printed their patterns on the ground.

This is Montreal

○·○·○·○·○·○·○·○·○·○·○·○·○·○·○·○·○·○·○·

A chatty crowd sat around circular tables spread across the room. Le Sainte-Élisabeth bar was buzzing with patrons, which we could not have guessed from the outside, as only the bouncer was in sight at the entrance. The room was compact, with tables close to each other as though everyone was part of the same big party. The bartender worked the counter, hidden behind an infinite collection of beer tap handles. He poured frosty beer in tall branded glasses and mixed drinks for his customers in choreographed movements, like an actor performing his masterpiece on a big stage.

"How is your family doing?" I asked.

"They're doing well. I got to see baby Mason," Karen said. "Did I tell you my older sister had a baby?" She studied the drinks menu in her hands. Bar lights reflected on her face and on the leather decor around us.

"Was baby Mason happy to see Auntie Karen?"

"He's so adorable!" She scrolled through her phone and showed me a few photographs of her and the baby.

She carried her nephew in the pictures, smiling with all her teeth. His angel face stared into the camera with wide eyes, probably wondering what was going on . . .

"Do you see yourself having kids of your own sometime?"

"Maybe," Karen sighed, a bit exasperated. "I don't have much of a social life where I live. You know that, right? I love my job, but life is quite lonely, I'd say."

"It doesn't have to be that way!"

"It's not that simple, Saba."

I changed the subject. "What have you been working on lately?"

"I'm working on a funding proposal," she said. "We developed this project to help rural farmers increase yields and financial security through crop insurance . . ."

A bald pianist sat in a corner playing, the sound muffled by the chitter-chatter of a crowd more absorbed by their conversations than live music.

"Well, that brings back a few memories of my former job. I left nonprofit work behind when I started my career in the private sector."

"Good for you!" Karen said. "You know what they say . . . we have to work ourselves out of a job." She smiled. "I'm still working on that."

"Karen, as broken as the current nonprofit landscape is, I think there will always be a role for philanthropy in this world. Corporate interests and the government can't fix it all."

"Speaking of which, Dan sent me an interesting article a week ago about reforming market capitalism," she said. "I'll forward it to you."

"You kept in touch with Dan after you left Kigali?"

"Yes, we chat once in a while," she said. "Personally, I'd love to see more resources go toward local grassroots organizations."

I unbuttoned my winter coat and threw it on top of Karen's, which she had put on a vacant chair.

"Hey, are you guys new to the city?" a young woman seated next to us interrupted. She had made eye contact with me too often not to say something. Our tables were close, and people could talk without overreaching.

The young woman wore a crop top, exposing her midriff, and sat with her group of friends. She introduced us to her companions, whose names I forgot on the spot. I remember being impressed by their careers, however. One, a classmate of hers, was a speech therapy major. Two of her other friends at the table had great jobs as well. One was a medical student at McGill University. The other was a computer scientist who had recently moved from Toronto to work with Bombardier, the Canadian aerospace company.

"You should join the conversation," the woman who first spoke to me said with a smile, almost as if she meant the opposite.

"What are you guys talking about?" I said, looking at the two guys who sat across from their female companions.

"Data privacy," one guy replied.

"Interesting topic!"

I bet I was better read than your average travel agent. Probably a way of compensating for my low-tier career path. My parents held strong opinions about what decent career choices were. Unfortunately for me, being a travel agent wasn't one of them. My career, just like my love life, had become a mystery on a good day and a problem that warranted an emergency family meeting on a bad one.

At every family dinner, party, or get-together, my family would ask why I didn't do things "like the others," why I didn't have a wife and kids, and why I didn't have a house to my name. These questions weren't just part of the conversation; they *were* the conversation! I had tried to laugh it off at first but had grown to resent them. Every time we got together, they made the same exasperating comments. These weren't questions meant to clarify or seek new information; they were a passive-aggressive way to apply social pressure on my life choices.

Sometimes I wanted to tell my family I was in love with Karen, but I didn't. I didn't tell my brother or sister that I'd asked Karen out. I needed the space to sort things out with her first. How could I have explained to my family that my love interest had asked me to wait for two years? It was too hard to justify, even harder to understand. Besides, they would have hated her for it, and I wanted to protect her from the potential drama until we were officially together.

"You guys should join our table," the woman sitting beside our table insisted. I turned to Karen to get a sense of what she thought.

"I don't mind joining them," Karen said.

"All right, let's do it!"

We pulled our chairs out and pushed tables together before sitting with the group of strangers we had just met. The woman who invited us immediately asked the group to play a board game and change the conversation.

We went through a round of Cards Against Humanity, which was placed on tables at the bar alongside other games to entertain guests.

In the meantime, Karen ordered a couple rounds of beer and a new plate of french fries for the group after she spontaneously helped herself to the food on our new friends' table.

As we went through rounds of Belgian ale, laughter from the group increased. One woman pulled her phone out of her pocket to look for more group games.

"Yes, let's play 'Never Have I Ever,'" she slurred, already tipsy from alcohol.

She flipped through prompts on her phone, specially designed to provide shock value, disturb sensibilities, and ease people into airing their most embarrassing vices and fantasies to the public.

Karen discreetly explained the rules to me at the beginning of each game. To everybody else, bar games were second nature, like playing football. Everybody knew the rules—everybody but me!

The rounds of booze facilitated the process. As if in a quasi-spiritual haze, everybody confessed their sins without shame or contrition, without the clarity of mind necessary to assign moral judgment or produce repentance, and without the usual priest and resulting Hail Mary.

"Let's hit the club, guys!" the strong-willed woman yelled to the group, sensing that the mood at our table had outgrown the low-key atmosphere at the bar. It was around midnight.

"Do you want to go out?" I looked at Karen with hesitation.

"That'd be fun."

"It's up to you, really," I said. "You're the one with an early plane to catch."

Karen was in town just for the day. She was flying back to Zambia, where she lived, through Montreal's airport just so we could meet and catch up.

"Come on, guys! Let's fuckin' go!" The young woman motioned for the table to stand before Karen and I could finish our deliberations.

"Do clubs open on a Wednesday night?" I said.

"Dude, where do you think you are?" She stared at me, confused, aggravated. Her eyes were glassy. "Dude, listen, listen..." The smell of beer breath hit my face as she yelled. "Listen to me! This is Montreal! You're in fuckin' Montreal! Every day is club day!"

After a few rounds of Never Have I Ever with this group, Karen and I realized our lives were boring, and we had some serious catching up to do. It was that or our friends were undoubtedly crazy. There was no in-between. We learned, among other disturbing facts, that we were the only ones who had never been to a strip club or had sex in a church.

We joined the group and headed to the club. The woman had convinced us that if there was a place on earth that could remedy our "lacking" life experiences, Montreal was that place. Despite her city streets bearing the names of biblical saints, everything seemed permissible in the "Party Capital of Canada!"

The Nightlife

o · o · o · o · o · o · o · o · o · o · o · o · o · o · o · o · o · o · o ·

The music echoed from a distance as we approached the nightclub in downtown Montreal. We got a hand stamp and checked into the coatroom to get the weight of heavy coats off our shoulders. Karen walked up the stairs behind the group, and I followed her. She was wearing a white sleeveless shirt tucked into tight jeans. Her faux-leather belt hugged her tiny waist tight, highlighting her natural curves.

I stopped and checked underneath my leather boots. My shoes stuck on the floor as I stepped up the stairs as if I were walking on freshly poured asphalt. Oily beer spills lingered on the floor. The lights grew dimmer, the noise intensified, and the music became almost deafening as we neared the end of the staircase. I couldn't tell if it was good or bad music. You can make nearly any song sound decent at that high volume.

Spotlights beamed from the ceiling in multiple colors, like laser weapons tearing through the room's darkness, lighting up the faces in red, blue, and purple. People in club attire swayed their bodies to the tune of the music, a frenetic beat from the DJ's turntables.

A strong smell of beer hit my nostrils as our group approached the crowd. Karen and I walked toward the dance floor behind everyone else. We stopped when the friends we'd met dissolved into an unruly crowd.

Girls were shuffle-dancing, sending their straightened hair flying at the rhythm of the loud, fast beat. One group of women danced together in a circle. A man enfolded another woman in his arms as they kissed. Yet another man was drinking tequila from the bottle and dancing by himself. Stoned to death, his mellow body responded to club music only through hand gestures, the only parts of his body he seemed to be able to still move . . .

The amount of beer we had consumed earlier and the intense tempo loosened the mood. Karen was grooving to the music, gently rocking her head. Her face shone through a rainbow of spotlights spinning from above the stage.

I was running out of my go-to moves when the DJ played Swedish House Mafia's "Don't You Worry, Child." It was one of my favorite songs, and a fresh gush of energy went through my body. I pulled Karen toward the stage and climbed up on the elevated platform to dance in the middle of a frenzied crowd.

This song summarized my story through its lyrics. I was unsure why I would want to dance to this melancholic song, but I did. The memory of Lake Tanganyika and the day I'd first asked Karen out flashed back to me. I blocked out the noise and thought of our first dance on the sandy shores of that lake. It was as if no time had been lost. This was the second time I had ever danced with her.

As the night aged, people danced with increasingly uncoordinated moves. You could almost tell each of the varying degrees of intoxication. Those who were worse off—the lightweights, as they call them—struggled to keep their bodies balanced on their feet or their beer from spilling on everyone around them.

I jumped off the stage and helped Karen carefully come down. At that point, I had forgotten about our friends. I looked around and couldn't find them. Delighted by this experience, I was glad they had invited us to join them, that a serendipitous moment had turned out pleasant. I scanned the room one last time, but still not seeing our friends, I zigzagged through the crowd toward the exit, pulling Karen's hand behind me.

o · o · o · o · o · o ·

MY BODY FELT WARM DESPITE the wintry air outside when we got out of the club.

We stopped at a McDonald's across the street. I let go of Karen's hand and keyed in my order and hers on the screen pad of a self-serve kiosk. A giant screen with menu options decorated the otherwise empty walls inside the fast-food restaurant. I tossed change in the coin cup that a fidgeting homeless man was shaking at us before we took a seat at one of the fixed metal tables.

"Did you have fun tonight?" I asked Karen as we sat at the rectangular table to eat. My head was still buzzing from prolonged exposure to loud music, as if someone had slapped me.

"I did!" Karen removed her winter hat and wrapped her curly hair in a top bun. "How are they not cold?" she said of a group of women waiting for their orders. Their revealing outfits defied the freezing temperatures outside.

It was around three o'clock in the morning. Homeless people had sought refuge from cold weather inside the McDonald's restaurant.

Yet the constant stream of human traffic from the club left the door open, making temperatures inside the building almost the same as outside.

"Thanks for making the trip north to meet up, Karen."

"Of course. I wanted to see you," she said before sinking her teeth into a double cheeseburger.

"By the way, you remember my colleague, Albert?" I said. "He'll travel to Zambia for work in about a month."

"Yeah?" she said. "I think I met him at your office the day we went hiking in the Virunga Mountains."

"I talked to him last night, and he's so excited he finally gets to go to Zambia. It was a bummer when he fell sick the last time he was supposed to go."

"Tell him to reach out when he's in town."

The fast-food restaurant faded into the background as I muted the voices of everyone around except Karen. Time was running out, and I wanted it to stop, to stand still just for the two of us. There were many things I wanted to tell Karen in person, like what we would do about jobs if we were together and where we would live in the short or the long term. She looked at me as if she could read my desire, crack my every thought, and feel my desperation. It was like she knew everything, and I needed to say no more.

"I'd like us to meet more often, you know," I said. "The problem is, I don't know how to make that happen." I shook my head.

"Don't beat yourself up too much, Saba."

"What do you say we look for jobs in the same city again?" I looked Karen in the eyes.

"You're not going to eat your burger?" My cheeseburger was still in its wrapper.

"My burger?" I said. "Oh, yeah, of course. I have a sensitive tooth that's been bothering me, but I'll use the other side."

"You should get your tooth checked."

"You're right. I'll see if I can get it fixed here, but it's no big deal." I unwrapped the burger. "Karen," I said, "why don't you move back to Kigali with me?" The time spent waiting for her while passing on other potential relationships weighed on my voice.

"Are you asking me to move in with you?"

"It'd be great to live in the same city!"

"My parents want me to come home, too, you know. They want me to move back stateside."

"They do?"

"Of all my siblings, I'm the only one who's ever been outside the United States," she said. "Both my sisters didn't even bother to move states when they got married."

"They both live in Georgia?"

"Not just that. They live in North Buckhead, Atlanta," she ranted with her mouth full. "In the same neighborhood we grew up in."

"You're such a rebel!"

"I think they made it harder for our parents to understand my choice of living so far away from everybody else."

"If it makes you feel better, my parents don't approve of my career choices either. They think I should've been an engineer, a medical doctor, for goodness' sake!" I chuckled. "But here I am—a travel agent!"

Karen smiled. I noticed she wore a beaded bracelet I had bought her a while back. She had kept the present over time and had put it on that night.

"Seriously, though, I think it'd be easier for you to find a job in Kigali if you moved back."

"I don't know, Saba. I want to stay in Zambia for a little while. My career is going well, and I want to see through the farmers' project I told you about before I move somewhere else," she said. "I've become attached to my work and the women I work with."

Part of me wanted to snap at Karen's reluctance to move closer to where I lived. I tried to tell her I was counting down the two-year mark she'd asked of me. I wanted to say she needed to show signs that she would hold up her end of the bargain.

However, the gaze of her big blue eyes cast a spell on me and convinced me the night was too serene to start a fight. I was in love. The love that sees the best in a person and magnifies it. The type that overlooks the bad and rationalizes it.

"You okay?" Karen asked, breaking the silence of my wandering thoughts.

"Yeah. Tired, I guess." I slowly massaged my left cheek; the gum underneath was hurting from chewing food. "Listen, Karen," I said, "think about what I said about moving back to Rwanda."

"It's almost certain I'll be at the KigaliUp music festival next summer," she said. "Why don't we meet then and talk about it." She rubbed her sleep-deprived eyes.

"All right," I said. "We'll have a lot to talk about next time we meet, huh? Next summer will mark two years since our trip to Bujumbura." I wiped my greasy fingers on a bunch of napkins and carefully folded the burger wrapper.

"That sounds about right." Karen smiled. "Should we head home? My plane is in about five hours."

The Dentist's Office

o·o·o·o·o·o·o·o·o·o·o·o·o·o·o·o·o·o·o·o·

A woman in her thirties sat motionless, leaning on the left armrest of her chair as she waited for her name to be called. Her chin sank into her palm as she stared blankly at a large painting on the wall: a framed oil on canvas depicting the sunrise over the city's harbor.

Strokes of colorful skies, ships docked at the port of Montreal, and silhouettes of the city's buildings graced the art piece. It was a beautiful painting that still somehow failed to lift the spirits in the waiting room.

The dentist's office is never like in the brochures, which depict smiling patients reading magazines and chatting while waiting to be seen by the doctor. In reality, the mood was rather somber and the conversations depressing.

"This is the fourth tooth they've removed," the woman said to me, pointing at her face and shaking a box of pills and papers in her hand. "How am I going to eat now?" she mumbled.

A dental assistant appeared through the door to exam rooms. "Do you have an appointment?" she acknowledged me. She closed the door, shutting out the whirring sound of a dental vacuum on the other side.

"No, I don't!" I said. "I have a tooth that's been hurting."

"Okay! Fill out this form." She handed me a patient identification form. "I'll be right with you."

The bulletin board on the wall reminded every visitor that bad oral hygiene damages both your smile and other parts of your body. A plaster model of dental composition lay on the table like a decorative piece of art: two biting jaws with teeth perfectly aligned.

"Le docteur est prêt pour vous, madame!" the dental assistant said to the other patient in French, telling her the doctor was ready for her.

I stayed behind in the waiting room as the assistant staff and the patient disappeared into another room. The environment suddenly became lonelier. Somehow, even a depressing conversation with a grumpy patient was better than no conversation at all. Only the sound of my knuckles cracking disturbed the calm.

Hopefully, the tooth will only need filling and I'll be in and out in a minute. Reassuring thoughts failed to calm my anxiety, however. People in medical gowns, the rehearsed smiles of medical staff, and the smell of disinfectant overcame my coolheaded senses. I hadn't felt this anxious since I'd gotten my first STD check after high school. Even though I had been chaste then, I'd grown paranoid while waiting for the results to come through. I thought I had caught an STD from a poorly sanitized blade at the barbershop or something. I didn't trust my barber's hygiene practices. My barber,

Naaj, was a childhood friend, but he took nothing seriously, including his job.

After a thirty-minute wait, I stepped into another room escorted by the dental assistant and sat on the dental chair. A spotlight shone on my face as the dentist tilted my jaw side to side to better look at my dental condition.

"When was the last time you saw a dentist?" he said.

"I don't know, doc. Maybe three years ago?"

"You have a cavity."

Another dental assistant entered the room and unwrapped a set of dental instruments. She spread them on a small silver platter like a cutlery platter in front of the dentist.

"I hate needles," I said as the dentist prepared the anesthesia.

"You will feel a little sting, just enough to numb you so we can clean and fill the tooth, okay?" the dentist muttered through his face mask. After injection, he waited for about seven minutes or so for the local anesthetic to take effect.

I closed my eyes and heard various instruments messing around my mouth. A small dental suction device drained the constant saliva flow triggered by the taste of topical anesthesia and the dentist's drill. I wondered why I hadn't waited to be back home to have my tooth checked.

Five minutes later, the dentist stopped the cleaning and pulled his drill out of my mouth. He pressed a button to raise the dental chair to an upright sitting position again.

"Saba! Is that your name?" he said with a clearer voice after removing his mask.

"Yes, sir!" I said, emulating his formal tone.

"We need to talk! You can rinse your mouth now." He pushed his dental instruments to the side.

He had barely cleaned my teeth and hadn't filled the tooth that had brought me here. I reached for the small plastic cup filled with water and mouthwash. My heart was racing.

I took one sip, then a second sip, and rinsed my mouth, stalling on what sounded like an uncomfortable discussion. I slowly wiped the side of my lips using the napkin they had fitted on my chest, but my numbed-up mouth was still drooling.

"Saba, do you have oral sex?"

"What?" I said. "No!" My eyes widened as I stared at him.

"Don't worry, it's common here," he said, surprised by my emphatic response.

"No, I don't!" I said. "Why would you ask me that?"

"There's a white spot at the back of your mouth. When was the last time you had a physical exam?"

"I'm not sure—ish been a while," I said, my shaky voice and insensate mouth struggling to sound out the *t*. Preventive health care wasn't a thing where I came from. You only go to the doctor when you get sick, not before.

"Doctors rarely look at your mouth in a physical exam anyway." He shrugged.

"Doc, are you positive this is something serious?"

"Well, we need to find out," he said. He walked across the room and brought a mirror to show me what looked like a white freckle at the back of my mouth on the soft palate area. "I want to transfer you to a colleague for a biopsy," the dentist said. "We can do that here, so you don't have to go to another medical office. My assistant will show you to another room, okay?"

"Wait," I said. "Did you say *biopsy*? Does that mean you suspect it might be cancer?"

"Yes, precisely," he said. "I know this is sudden, but I suggest we check the tissue first, and we can take care of your tooth afterward, okay?"

"Is it a long procedure?"

"No," he said, "it's a quick and simple procedure."

The dentist chatted with his assistant as I waited for them to sort out the logistics for the procedure. A massive photograph decorated the wall—a picture of Montreal's Olympic stadium. I wondered why I was in a dentist's chair and not out there sightseeing and having fun, but I didn't have an answer.

The dental assistant wheeled me to a different room at the clinic with my dentist in pursuit. A face mask covered my dentist's head, enhancing his eyebrows and the gaze of his eyes peeking over the light blue fabric.

The surgeon came into the room in a stereotypical outfit accompanied by two nurses. He was in a blue gown, his hands in his pocket, and a stethoscope hung around his neck. My dentist explained what needed to be done as the surgeon quietly nodded.

Before long, one nurse covered my eyes with a transparent pair of glasses for protection. A few minutes later, another nurse brought what looked like a laser gun and handed it to the surgeon.

Everything was going so fast. When I saw the laser gun, I swallowed the welling saliva in my mouth with a nervous gulp. The surgeon took the instrument and pointed it inside my wide-open mouth to sample the tissue that caused concern.

The smell of my flesh burning from a laser scalpel sent shivers down my body. It wasn't until that point that I realized my life might be in serious trouble.

"Your patient form says that you don't live in Montreal. Is that right?" the surgeon asked. "You should stay in the city for a few days to make sure you get the results. We should get the biopsy results in about a week."

Later, I stepped out of the building and stumbled onto the snow-covered walkway outside the clinic. My eyes grew watery and then welled over, tears flowing down my freezing cheeks, and I let them. I tightly tucked my hands in the deep pockets of my winter coat as I contemplated what had just happened and what would happen to my life if the test results confirmed what the doctor feared.

o · o · o · o · o · o ·

THE WEATHER HAD APPLIED A white-and-grayish filter to the city's landscape. Piles of snow sat silently on the edges of wet pathways. The few trees in sight wore dull colors and stood dwarfed by gigantic concrete buildings that loomed like shadows.

My thoughts raced at the speed of my walking pace, looking for answers to my potential problem, to no avail. That dreaded moment when the best explanation you could give yourself is "I don't know." The prospect of dealing with an incurable disease was like fighting an invisible bully who repeatedly punches you in the face but whom you cannot punch back.

My mind became blank and tuned out, only focused on the crunchy sound beneath my feet. That and the occasional beeping noise from cars driving were the only sounds tearing through the silence on the street.

As I walked around, tall buildings stared at me like crows perched on a tree.

I walked past Notre-Dame Street and took a right on St. Paul Street in Old Montreal, where more people were out and about. Strangers walked up and down the cobblestone path, as unaware of my fears as I was of theirs. They were probably carrying their own pains, worries, and unanswered questions. Their physical proximity somehow offered a little comfort and much-needed distraction.

Modern shops hid behind old buildings marked by medieval-style guild signs and lamps. As the locals call it, Rue Saint-Paul is the oldest street in Montreal and a must-see spot for first-time visitors.

I walked around until I got to one of the public benches over-looking the Notre-Dame Basilica. I sat.

Tourists took pictures of themselves nearby with the two-tow-ered church building in the background. From a distance, a street artist performed tricks in the open space surrounded by an intrigued group of young women somehow enjoying ice cream in the cold weather.

I reached down, and my ungloved hands burned as I touched the cold snow on the ground. I scooped a pile of snow, mashed it into a snowball, and slammed it on the ground.

"Sorry!" I waved in apology to a passerby whom I'd almost hit with the splashing snowball. He threw a concerned look at me and stopped walking!

"I'm sorry, man," I said again, but the man didn't walk away. Instead, he stood there looking at me with interest.

"Hey, are you okay?" he asked. His winter scarf hung low from his neck, exposing a clergy shirt underneath his coat.

"Yeah, I'm fine," I said. "Are you a priest?"

"Yes," he said. "I live in Quebec, but I am visiting Montreal." He came closer, standing in front of me. "So, what is bothering you so much that you're throwing snowballs at strangers?"

I leaned back on the wooden park bench and set my right ankle over my left knee in a leg clamp position. With a full head of hair, the priest seemed to be in his early forties. He had ditched the usual ankle-length soutane for a more casual look. Only his clergy shirt and a cross pendant hanging from his neck gave away his religious affiliation.

"My name is Father Dion," he said. "What's your name?"

"Saba! My name is Saba."

"That is a beautiful name."

"It means 'seven' in Swahili—the figure of perfection! That's what my mom would always say. She was proud of that name. She insisted the name was her idea, not Dad's. She wasn't too fond of his surname, so she gave a different last name to one of their kids. My parents had high hopes when they named me." I smiled.

"Let me ask you something, Father Dion. Have you always been a man of faith? I mean, how did you decide to become a priest?"

"That is a great question, Saba." He sat on the bench beside me and interlocked his hands. "I grew up in a Catholic family but never took religion seriously, until I was eighteen years old."

"What happened?"

"My younger brother, the youngest in our family, unexpectedly passed away at age fifteen."

"That's horrible!"

"Yeah, my conversion came through a tragic event, unfortunately."

"Sorry to hear that. I know people cope with tragic events differently. It must have been a shock to your family."

"'Good night' were the last words he said to me. It was after his school exam, on the following day, that he collapsed while playing soccer with other kids." Father Dion sat still; his eyes fixed in front of him.

"I'm so sorry to hear that. What a tragedy!"

"My family was never the same after that incident—my mother in particular. I was the only one at home when they called to say he collapsed. It was around one thirty p.m. on a summer day. I called my mother and told her they were taking him to the hospital. She left work and got fruit from a grocery store, my brother's favorite snack, before racing to the hospital to check on him. I still remember the school official's stoic voice when I called him again to ask how my younger brother was doing. 'It's over,' he said. 'He's dead.'"

The sad melody of a violin played outside the church building. A street performer sawed at the strings, his instrument tucked between his shoulder and neck. A gust of chilly wind blew across my face, and I lowered my winter hat to shield my ears.

Father Dion continued to recount the horrifying story of his loss. I had never heard a priest share such a personal story, and I wasn't sure what to do. I simply sat there, silent, listening.

"Faced with mortality, I had to find an answer to death before I could live again. Faith and devotion to God was the answer!" he said.

"I am happy you found a way to move forward, Father Dion."

"Well, almost as shocking as my brother's sudden passing was that we moved on. The world will always move on! Anyway, whatever is bothering you, I pray God gets you through it, my friend."

"Earlier today, I was at the hospital, and the doctor told me I might have a serious illness. If his medical suspicions come true, my life will be in trouble," I said. "Not that it solves anything, but coming here and being around people was my way of getting my mind off that."

"You see this church here and people taking pictures?" Father Dion swept his arm across the scene before us. "This church represents more than architectural genius. After all, those who first built it didn't mean it to be primarily a tourist destination. They built it because their congregation had outgrown the earlier church building. For them, it was a place of worship and prayer. It still is."

I gazed at the historic church in front of us as Father Dion explained its history.

Blue-lilac neon lights illuminated her three arched doors built underneath the H-shaped church structure. Three snow angels floated above each entrance like knights standing guard at the gates of heaven.

Aware of their limits and flaws, the people of the ancient community of this city had embraced the divine for atonement and spiritual nourishment. I could hear their silent faith in the providence of God ringing loud from the two bell towers elevated above the Gothic structure. They had carved their eternal hopes on the cross, which Maisonneuve, the city's founding father, planted atop Mont-Royal for all to see. These monuments were like a letter they wrote for future generations to read.

Like Father Dion, the early community had turned to faith when they woke up to life's biggest illusion: the belief that what is today will always be.

"It was great to meet you, Saba!" Father Dion checked his wristwatch underneath the long sleeve of his winter coat. "You seem like a good man. If I may, I'd like to pray for you before I leave."

I nodded.

"In the Name of the Father, the Son, and the Holy Spirit . . ." He drew the Trinitarian sign on his forehead and chest. I bowed my head as he prayed for faith in God, health, and good fortune, in that order.

"Thanks, Father Dion," I said as he stood from the bench. "I wouldn't say I'm a man of prayer, but I really enjoyed our discussion."

"Everybody prays, my friend," he said. "Everybody prays in the end, but the wise pray before the end!"

He wrapped his scarf around his neck and walked away.

At a Tiki Bar

o·o·o·o·o·o·o·o·o·o·o·o·o·o·o·o·o·o·o·

G in and tonic, please!" I said to the bartender.

"Single or double?" he responded, mixing drinks behind the counter with both hands. He was wearing a T-shirt that exposed his arms: tattoos crawled up the entire length of one like aggressive roots on a tree.

"Make it double."

I handed him twelve Canadian dollars and slipped a few coins I had into the tip jar at the counter. When I'd arrived, happy hour rates were over. I'd stayed inside that day until about 7 p.m., when I couldn't see the sunlight outside my window. I'd even traded the complimentary breakfast at my hostel for a protein bar to stay in bed—a decision I'd later regretted when I'd learned my hostel had made flaky croissants and chocolate éclairs for all its guests that morning.

The bar was in the basement of my hostel and had ample space to accommodate a good-sized crowd. People were scattered around the room, chatting and drinking, surrounded by bare brick walls. Fur coats and winter jackets hung behind chairs and barstools. A thousand lamps dangled from the ceiling in all shapes, sizes, and colors, but somehow the room was still dimly lit. Lights shone with low brightness, intentionally half as luminous as possible. The purple lights shone brightest of them all. Their glow burned with intensity, forcing the room to a grape-violet shade.

I stirred the ice rocks in my glass and placed the straw on a napkin on the counter. The burning smell of alcohol rushed through my nose as I sipped the drink.

One woman, who looked to be in her midtwenties, sat alone on the left side of the counter. I thought of talking to her but realized she wasn't alone; the bartender chatted with her whenever he wasn't attending to his multiple patrons. The young woman wore a leather jacket, and her hair concealed her face like a dark curtain; only when the bartender approached her with another drink on the house or a joke did she tuck her hair behind her ear, exposing her heavily made-up face.

Another couple sat on my right at the other end of the counter. The man and his date had turned their chairs toward each other, and their legs were conveniently touching.

A group of three women—slender brunettes with dark eyes and olive skin tone—sat in plushy chairs around a table. One girl caught my wandering eye as I surveyed the room. I glanced away and pretended to look at my empty glass. I peeked back at her, and she was still looking at me, smiling as if she had just won a power contest. She broke eye contact and dropped her gaze, then lifted her eyes to look at me from under her lashes, like she would let me win one and even up the game . . .

A few men stood nearby with drinks in their hands. They threw sheepish looks at the group of girls between sips of alcohol, hoping a few more shots of hard liquor would summon the manliness they needed to walk over and talk to them. One of them burst into uncontrolled laughter and raised his voice above the noise and the music at the bar, but no one seemed to care except his friends, who laughed with him. The bar was like a temple where the booze and music kicked off the ritual of people letting loose and washing away their worries and shortfalls in alcohol.

The music mix failed to pin a specific vibe down. Somehow, the bar manager thought it wise to let guests at the international hostel change the bar's playlist at will based on their personal tastes. A mishmash of music genres alternated from loudspeakers around the room: rap songs from Quebec, Turkish music, and a few exotic tunes familiar to only two or three people who had picked them and sang along.

The only active entertainment at the bar was a pool table; a few people played. The small screen on the wall that displayed lyrics on Karaoke Mondays was dark, as it was Friday night.

One man at the pool table finally got the courage to wave the group of girls over for a game of pool. When the women eventually joined, the men congregated around the pool table took off a layer of clothing as the temperature in the room rose a few degrees Celsius.

"Voulez-vous jouer? I am Moira." The girl who had looked at me earlier came over and asked if I wanted to play pool with them. She spoke to her friends in Canadian French and switched to English when addressing other guys at the bar. But she correctly guessed I spoke French.

"Let's play pool, ladies. You bring energy back!" one guy said with a thick accent. He was from Mexico, we learned after he introduced himself.

The group formed two mixed teams, with me and Moira as one. One of Moira's friends, Nadine, played with the Mexican guy against our team.

Determined to keep the temperature in the room above freezing levels, the girls took over the playlist, the last thing that needed to change to make the ambience at the bar more satisfying. They chose upbeat songs, songs that could make it on the top one-hundred list on the Billboard chart.

Moira wore dark eyeliner that perfectly complemented her eyes and complexion. Each pool shot she took looked like a performance show. Moira whispered in her girlfriend's ear and nonchalantly giggled about it. She slowly bent over the pool table in her revealing mesh crop top and gyrated up and down to the music beat, like a pole dancer, every time she made or missed a shot. She wasn't just attractive; she commanded attention, and she loved it.

As the game went on, more people from the bar congregated around the pool table.

"C'est ton tour de jouer," Moira said—my play was up. She grabbed my phone from my hand and offered to keep it as I played, and I let her.

She opened the camera, stuck her tongue out, and took a selfie before typing her phone number below the image and saving it in my contacts. Her fingernails sparkled, and each finger had a ring on it, except for the ring finger.

Moira handed me her glass of Belgian craft beer to hold when her turn to play came around again.

"So, what are you doing after the game?" Moira said in English this time.

"I'm just hanging out here. I don't feel like going out today."

"Celui-ci m'a l'air un peu trop sérieux!" She told her friend that I looked too uptight, unconcerned that I could hear her.

I took a step back and looked at the pool table, visualizing the direction I should send the ball in as the game came down to the last shot. Moira stood close to me and studied the layout of the balls too. She gestured with her hand to suggest how I should strike.

I carefully aimed at the black eight ball sitting on the flat green surface of the pool table and took the shot. My right hand twitched at the last second and the shot missed, which sent the white cue ball rolling into a pocket instead. The crowd groaned in disappointment.

An argument broke out about the scratch rules. Nadine's teammate argued they only needed to put the cue ball behind the head string. Moira and I argued that the opposing team should use a tougher cushion or indirect shot on the last play. Curiously enough, Nadine agreed with us. She insisted her team win in the fairest ways, but her partner disagreed.

"Let them have it! That's an easy shot to make," Nadine yelled at her teammate.

Before we could settle on the rules, Nadine's teammate took the shot directly and sank the eight ball into one pocket.

"Game over! We won!" He looked at Nadine, perplexed at her lack of enthusiasm for their win. "You are on my team. You should be happy!"

"Comment on dit tricheur en anglais?" Unimpressed, Nadine asked Moira what English word to use, then remembered. "Cheater!" Nadine yelled at her teammate before Moira could respond. "You're a cheater!"

"Guys, take it easy! Fair play, you guys won!" I said.

Moira, Nadine, and her other friend immediately went out a back door to smoke. I retreated to a nearby stool and sat there as other people at the bar took over the next game of pool.

My body felt warmer as I finished my third gin and tonic. Despite the drama at the end, playing pool with this group had somehow lifted my mood. I felt light, carefree, and happier. My health anxieties were no more, and my worries were gone, not by spiritual contemplation this time, but by the soothing effect of gin and unattached women.

Deep down, I was exhausted, starved of affection and weary of waiting for what could be a declaration of my imminent death. I was tired of waiting for Karen to determine where we stood, tired of letting my hopes of intimacy with a woman hang on a loose promise of a relationship months down the road. I wanted to turn the page, move on with my life, and build something new with someone else.

Father Dion's touching story a day earlier and the ensuing thoughts about embracing faith were still vivid in my mind, however. I didn't want to discount my serendipitous encounter with him. Yet the same existential questions continued to bother me: questions of love, meaning, purpose, and destiny, questions about faith and what happens when we die. What if meeting Father Dion was a sign from God and Him trying to reach out with answers to my questions? I didn't know what a sign from God would even look like.

"God, give me a sign if you want me to wait." I whispered to myself in prayer for the first time. I don't know if my prayer was sincere or if I was acting strangely because of the alcohol I consumed.

Still, for the first time, I spoke to God. I had learned a few sentences from my old roommate, Kamana. He liked to pray before every meal—often out loud, as if he wanted me to hear what he was saying. I remember his prayers were casual and endearing. He called God "Papa," as if God were his own dad or something.

I heard a rhythmic click-clack on the floor behind me. Moira's leather boots knocked against the hardwood floor as she strode in my direction.

"My girlfriends and I are going to another bar," she said. "You want to join?"

"Where're you going?"

"I will show you." She swiped through directions on her phone, gently bobbing her head to the alternative rock music playing at the bar. She held up her phone screen when she found the bar's location on the map app.

"This is where we're going." She stepped closer and showed me pictures of the place. Standing, she was just as tall as I was sitting on the barstool.

Moira leaned in closer, gently scrolling through the images in front of my eyes. She shifted until her chest touched my arm and her nipple brushed my left triceps. The swell of her boob pressed against my arm, stirring every nerve in my body. She backed up a bit as if nothing had happened, then moved closer and touched me again for a few more seconds.

We took a cab and headed north, about a twenty-minute drive from the city center. I sat in the front seat while Moira, Nadine, and the other girl, whose name I don't recall, took the back seat.

Moira restored in me something I didn't know I had lost. Preoccupied with death and hung up on a pseudo-relationship with Karen, I had forgotten how to be present. I'd been asking myself the wrong question. I wondered what I would do today if I were to die tomorrow, instead of asking what I would do today if I were to live tomorrow . . .

Our cab driver, Muhammad, played "Jesus Breaks Every Chain" on his car stereo as we drove toward Little Italy.

o · o · o · o · o · o ·

WE MADE OUR WAY INTO a busy tiki bar in a cozy neighborhood. Wooden masks and carvings decorated the walls. Rainbow-colored balls shone from the ceiling and pulsed at the rhythm of a subtle tribal drum playing in the background.

The bartender acknowledged Moira and her friends as we took the counter seats. Liquor bottles lined the cabinet behind the bartender, below wooden artifacts on higher shelves. I looked a bit out of place in my outfit and wondered what spot this was. Never had I seen such decor at a bar. The theme and bamboo ornaments gave it a tropical atmosphere, even as we were in the middle of Canadian winter.

After browsing through the cocktail list for a minute, I asked the bartender to suggest something.

Before long, she slid a massive icy glass in front of me; a blue flame burned on top of it. When I saw it, my head jittered backward as if the flame would set my face on fire. I carefully removed the small flame container from my drink with two fingers, put it to the side, and tasted the creamy cocktail.

"What alcohol content is in this drink?" I said after taking the first sip.

"A lot." Moira shrugged. "That's the Zombie cocktail!"

"Ha! And you're just telling me now?"

"Whatever! Cheers!" We clinked our glasses.

A ukulele melody played, barely rising above the noise at the bar. Moira had slung her winter coat over the barstool backrest. She sat facing me with her bare knee touching the side of my leg.

"Saba, have you ever been to a tiki bar before?"

"No, I have not," I said. "This is my first time."

Moira pulled me by my jacket and whispered in my ear.

"Don't worry," she said, "you'll have all your first times with me tonight!"

CHAPTER 5

Visit to the District

o·o·o·o·o·o·o·o·o·o·o·o·o·o·o·o·o·o·o·o·

It was a warm day in March, and the cherry trees were nearing peak bloom. They looked as happy as the people were to regain warmth and color as winter gave way to spring.

I poured whole milk over boiling coffee and held my warm mug with both hands. My fingertips stroked the words *Hakuna Matata* printed on my coffee mug.

I sipped and sipped again to irrigate my throat, which was dry from the heating in my studio apartment. The building still hadn't changed the air of the central heating and cooling system from hot to cold.

I stood next to my dining table resting against the wall, and my eyes wandered outside my window.

A forest with red, green, and yellow foliage hid the blue sky above Rock Creek Park. It was my morning routine to stare outside my apartment window with a cup of coffee, immersing my soul in this view. This sight of nature reminded me of my home country. The first time I'd looked out the window after I'd moved in, I'd thought something was missing, but I couldn't figure out what. It wasn't until a few days later that I'd realized the pleasant sight of nature was without its familiar sounds.

There was no dawn chorus in the morning, no waves of melodies from various wildlife characters outside. There were no chirping birds, rooster's sunrise song, house sparrows, or weaver birds. Instead, the wailing sirens, honking car horns, and shattering glass crushed by the garbage truck welcomed the day.

I picked up the bag of coffee beans I had bought at the local farmers' market and put my nose to the top, squeezing the bottom. A gentle aroma rushed through my nostrils, and I nodded in approval. Not as strong as Rwandan coffee, but still good strong coffee.

The cooking pan sat in the sink, caked with the remains of the spaghetti and meatball dinner I had made the day before. I had postponed handwashing it as it was too big to fit in my full dishwasher.

I had been working and living in Washington, DC, for three months. Mr. Sadiki had extended my stay in North America so I could build partnerships with local travel and tour companies. I was to work from DC for three additional months before returning to Kigali via Asia.

This was the longest I had lived away from my home country. The culture shock had hit me hard. It had left me disoriented, struggling to adapt to different social and visual clues.

What had me feeling out of place wasn't that everything looked big here, from meal portions to building structures. It wasn't the eccentric options at grocery stores, where endless aisles insisted that even drinking water came in flavors and "natural" dyes of every color known to man. It wasn't even that there were more baby dogs than baby humans walking the city streets, or the many psychic shops that freaked me out. Instead, the intense sense of individualism was the issue, the paradox of living free and isolated simultaneously. Life here was fast-paced, ambitious, and independent. Certainly more productive, but also less social and lonelier than my home country in Africa.

Whether the gains in productivity are worth the trade-off in social relations, I don't know. I read somewhere that social isolation is a more significant health risk than smoking, diabetes, or lack of physical activity.

Is chasing a career and enhanced productivity at the expense of a social and family life worth it? Life in the States was like a drug commercial: the benefits and gains are loudly lauded before a sneaky list of deadly side effects pops up.

My apartment door shut behind me as I walked down the carpeted hallway. Before exiting the building, I stopped to talk to Martha, our concierge. Her congenial presence was impossible to ignore, even in a city where everyone limits small talk with strangers to a strict minimum.

A metro transit officer stood outside the entrance to the trains in her uniform, with a bag of chips in her hand. The metro wasn't busy—there was no rush of people going down the escalators to the metro cars, as morning rush hour had passed.

People on the metro ditched the empty seats and held on to the car railings instead. Their bowed heads rocked back and forth as the metro car sledded over the rails with a screeching sound. Everyone looked down at their cell phones or shoes, their necks hanging so they would avoid eye contact with other commuters. Their social etiquette overruled the need to maintain a healthy spine position.

I found Elise, Dan's girlfriend, sitting beside a young couple on the stairs near the museum's entrance.

"So great to see you, Saba!"

"Sorry I'm late."

"Do you live far from here?" Elise said after a long hug.

"It's not that far," I said, sitting beside her. "I got caught up in discussion with our concierge."

"How many times have you been to the Mall at this point?"

"Too many to count. I come here often," I said. "The city is very walkable, and I like to be outside. I haven't been able to visit this museum, though. There's usually a long line to get your hands on admission tickets."

The couple sitting next to us discussed their visit to the National Museum of African American History and Culture.

"Do you have a black friend?" the woman asked her companion.

"I don't know how to respond to that question," he said. "Asking if I have a black friend seems like an oxymoron."

"What?" The woman gave him a confused look. Elise and I kept quiet, secretly eavesdropping on this conversation, wondering how it would end.

"You identify someone by their physical features when you don't know them. Meaning when you're not friends," he said with hand gestures, clarifying his thoughts.

"Well, I think you can say that even when you're friends," the woman said.

"When you meet a person for the first time, the only thing you see is their appearance: a tall black man, a skinny white woman with red hair, an Asian woman. However, once you get to know them, they're no longer 'the Asian woman' or 'the black man.' They're Amy and AJ or whatever their names are. I don't like that question because it reverses this beautiful friendship process and turns Amy back into 'the Asian woman' and AJ into 'the black guy.' It turns them into strangers again."

"There's an interesting take." She smiled. "So, you don't?"

We stood up and started walking toward the west end of the Mall. The National Mall, also called America's Front Yard, is a wide greensward and home to the most iconic landmarks of Washington, DC.

Elise and I both wore blue and white, except in reverse order, almost making it appear as if we were wearing high school uniforms. She walked around in her blue jeans and a light gray sweatshirt, and I had on my blue Washington, DC–branded hoodie and soft gray pants.

"It was my childhood dream to come to America," I told her. "I have felt connected to the US since I was a kid. Being here is surreal."

"Why do you think that is?"

"Well, America's influence is everywhere. Movies, music, food. Even the most remote villages in Africa get their Coca-Cola shop before power lines and water pipes."

"Our iconic exports!" She smiled.

A gentle wind blew on our faces.

"So you have the Washington Monument in the middle. The White House and Jefferson Memorial are on either side of the Washington Monument, and the Lincoln Memorial is on the other end," I explained, pointing at landmarks like a flight attendant going through the safety protocols before takeoff.

"Don't forget the Capitol Building on the opposite end!"

Elise had grown up in a small town called Oxford, Mississippi, before moving to New York City for college. After graduating from Columbia University with a performing arts major and an international relations minor, Elise had moved to Rwanda with her boyfriend, Dan. She worked for one of the rare performing arts schools in the country called City Arts.

With her soft-spoken personality, Elise struck me as someone who was gentle but could be blunt and persistent. The dichotomy of her demeanor had permeated her dance performance the few times Karen, Dan, and I had attended her shows together. Her dance routines involved both graceful piqué turns and bursting leaps.

We took pictures of the Lincoln Memorial alongside hordes of tourists and locals who came to catch an early glimpse of the blooming cherry trees and admire the monuments. I could see myself in their inquisitive eyes; we were all overjoyed and overwhelmed by so much to see.

Monuments in Washington, DC, project an inescapable aura of grandeur that inspires awe and fascination. America's landmarks are oversized and grand, like towers erected so the entire world could see what the pinnacle of civilization looks like. They are symbols not of perfection, however, but of progress. They are emblems of a nation daring to be free and aspiring to greatness, of a country that was led to a better place by the women and men who called her home. The statue of President Lincoln sat on the western end of the Mall in a Doric temple, watching over the nation he once governed.

In West Potomac Park stood another historic man, Reverend Martin Luther King Jr., who inspired America to move past its racial divides. In his honor, the people of this nation erected a memorial not far from where he gave his most famous speech, "I Have a Dream."

In the shadows of the towering figures who'd walked these streets in decades past was a young and hustling crowd hoping to lay their brick on the edifice of this nation. Ambitious twenty- and thirtysomethings interned or worked at one of the alphabet soup organizations in town.

"How is Dan doing?" I asked Elise, who walked beside me.

"A bit bummed he couldn't join me on this trip, but he was busy with his business consulting job," she said, dodging tourists driving Segways on the sidewalk.

"Tell him I said hi. I haven't seen him in a while . . ."

We walked past the World War II memorial, its granite pillars adorned with wreaths, and the Rainbow Pool before stopping for a mandatory picture at the White House.

It wasn't until we spent a couple hours at the Mall that we left and headed toward Seventeenth and I Street Northwest. It's easy to find your way around the city. Lettered and numbered roads cross each other in a grid pattern, and significant avenues carry the names of US states.

"Elise, how long have you and Dan been together?"

"For about four years now."

"That's quite some time. Thinking about getting married yet?"

Elise turned her head and looked at me before answering. "Married?" she said. "Where did that come from? We aren't thinking about that."

"I don't know," I said. "Because you've dated for a while, I assume that would be the next move, right?"

"It's not a priority for us, really. Are you and Karen getting married?" she shot back.

"I wish! Karen and I aren't even dating. I like her, but we still need to determine where we stand. But there's something about committing to another person that I find noble."

"Well, Dan is my boyfriend. That's our commitment!" Elise smiled.

"Yes, but I mean long-term commitment. You know, like that Roman general who sank his own ship after arriving on the island he was about to conquer, to prevent his men from retreating? Like sailing without a life vest, pledging to float the ship or go down with it, so to speak."

"Ha! That's not how it works! That's an unhealthy view of relationships if you ask me. Do you think Karen wants to get married and settle down?"

"I don't know what Karen wants, to be honest with you. I hope to find out soon enough, though."

"Sounds like a lot of pressure to me," she said, giving me another concerned look. "You should take it easy, Saba. Enjoy life and have fun. If something develops over time, so be it. If not, that's okay too."

"I don't know, Elise. For a long time, I have been waiting for her. I think it's driving me crazy," I said. "I've been dealing with a lot lately."

"What happened?"

My head dropped, and I stared at my own steps as we walked up Seventeenth Street.

"I had a cancer scare in Montreal about three months ago, and I'm still shaken by the whole situation."

"No kidding! Did you do a biopsy?"

"Yeah, I did! And the results were almost comical," I said. "I waited for the results to arrive with a lot of anxiety. When they did, the doctor told me that the tissue they thought was cancerous was just a cut by something else, like a french fry or a chip."

"Thank goodness!" Elise said. "It must have been such a relief!" She rubbed my back.

"I didn't tell Karen, though, so keep it between us for now. These are things you talk about in person."

"Speaking of Karen," she said, "I'm excited that she will be back in Kigali soon! Dan told me she's visiting this summer."

"Dan has been in touch with Karen?"

"Yeah, they've been in touch," she said casually. "Dan's been thinking about expanding his business operations to Zambia, so Karen's been helping him develop local connections."

Since I'd last met her in Montreal, getting news from Karen had become increasingly difficult. Not that she wasn't reaching out or texting. We were still in touch, but the length of our conversations had become shorter and shorter as weeks went by. I thought this might have been because we knew each other well and had exhausted the conversations. After all, the more we talked, the fewer new things we had to discover about each other. But it was more than that. It was the annoying games she played that bothered me.

Karen would send a text message saying she missed me and wanted to catch up soon. But when I would try to set up a definitive video date with her, she would tell me to check in during the weekend. When the weekend came, Karen would come up with an excuse, like "I need to catch up with my mom" or "I'm doing a video chat with my sister and baby Mason." She would hit me with something family-related, something she knew I couldn't argue with or object to. We would be silent for a couple weeks after that, and then Karen would text me again, and the same cycle would repeat.

It seemed like she wasn't ready to have me but didn't want to lose me either. That last part kept me hopeful, however. Given enough time, she would come around, and we would pick up where we left off. I just knew it.

The Wedding's After-Party

○·○·○·○·○·○·○·○·○·○·○·○·○·○·○·○·○·○·○·

My greasy fingers grabbed chips and brought them to my mouth before I wiped them against a stash of napkins at the table. Hung on the basement's concrete columns, four TV screens silently glared overhead. Two played C-SPAN and the others showed sports commentary with closed captioning.

Screams of "woo-hoo" and clapping erupted as the pianist played the intro to one of the bar favorites. He played with the audience's emotions and hesitated to speak into his microphone, teasing the crowd into a frenzy as he raised the anticipation to greater heights. He whispered the first words into the microphone as if he were sweet-talking a woman he was deeply in love with.

At the top of their lungs, the crowd sang together like a chorus, except unworried about hitting the right notes or organizing vocal parts into soprano, tenor, alto, and bass. The passion mattered most, and the good times the song evoked.

"What are you writing?" Elise asked as I scribbled on a piece of paper.

We had secured a couple of barstools next to the piano. I sat on the one with a torn leather seat, squeezed between Elise and another woman who had purple hair and was wearing a T-shirt that read Stop Fascism in bold letters.

"Guess what song I am requesting?"

"'I Love Rock 'n' Roll,'" Elise sang.

"No! Not that one," I said. "I'm requesting 'Wonderful Tonight' by Eric Clapton."

Elise was in a Friday-night mood, almost on a par with the bar crowd. Smiling, she swung her head back and forth to the song's rhythm as I observed her with interest.

I slid the folded paper behind the queue and put a couple of one-dollar bills in the glass bowl in front of the pianist. The piano lid was down, and beer bottles and glasses of wine had turned the edges of the giant piano into a bar table. The pianist didn't seem to mind the intrusion. Quite the contrary—he fed off people's energy as he performed.

The pianist sat behind his microphone. He had loosened the top buttons on his white shirt. The long line of uneven pieces of paper in front of him didn't seem to overwhelm him; he simply separated the pile of songs he had played from new requests. His tip jar overflowed with dollar bills.

"How was the wedding?"

"I loved it!" Elise answered. "I've known Emily, my friend who got married, since middle school."

"I'm glad you got to be at her wedding," I said. "It's rare to keep a friend for that long." I finished my beer. I drank faster when the music was playing.

Dim lights hung from a naked ceiling with exposed pipes. The new trend at restaurants and bars in town started as a practical trade-off for easier maintenance and repairs. Over time, exposed pipes slowly became an acceptable option for ceiling finishes.

"You should have joined me as my plus-one, you know," she leaned in and said into my ear to beat the loud music mixed with a hundred bar conversations. The artist played classic songs from memory and had an iPad screen fixed before him to search for lyrics and chords of less familiar requests.

"I'm not a big fan of large family gatherings with people I don't know."

Elise paused and sipped her beer. "Well, you know me, Saba! Besides, a wedding is more than a family gathering."

The music's vibrations echoed from loudspeakers to our ears and bodies.

"I prefer to meet here at the piano bar," I said. "The music is good, don't you think?"

Elise finished her drink, tilting her head backward and emptying the contents in one go. Meanwhile, her glowing eyes looked at me, yet she didn't say another word.

The Piano Bar was on M Street in Georgetown, or, as I called it, the Champs-Élysées of Washington, DC.

City streets in DC, with their leveled row houses, looked like those of a European city. The European influence dates to the city's early days. Pierre L'Enfant, a French American architect and native of Paris, designed the original plan for the nation's capital in 1791.

The European vibe can be seen through the moderate height of DC's buildings, her cosmopolitan population, her strong coffee culture, and even her smoking habits—if you replaced cigarettes with marijuana joints, that is.

We left the bar at about 11:30 p.m. We walked from Thirty-Third and M Streets toward the waterfront, where the Potomac River separates Washington, DC, from neighboring Virginia.

It was a calm night, and the click of Elise's high heels resonated as we made our way toward the river. A roaring motorcycle suddenly perturbed the night with its accelerating noise as we turned right on Wisconsin Avenue.

When we arrived at the waterfront, we sat on the granite steps facing the river as if we were in a stadium, admiring a spectacle outdoors.

Elise, a Southern girl with a New York City fashion sense, had fitted a black cocktail dress on her slender figure and tied it off with cherry-red lipstick. However, the daylong wedding ceremony she had attended earlier that day had softened the sharp edges of her makeup lines. The refined scent of her perfume had mixed with the smell of alcohol from the celebration.

Despite the small public lights planted along the promenade, shadows stretched across the granite steps. They almost hid the faces of the only other couple sitting on the spacious staircase overlooking the river, but I could still tell they were making out.

The quacking ducks that usually floated on the water's surface and waited for people to throw them food had retreated into their nests. I could hear only the sound of crickets and frogs.

Elise sat next to me with her legs crossed. She removed her bobby pins and let her hair down.

"Thanks for taking me to the piano bar, Saba."

"Glad you liked it."

The wind caressed our bodies as we sat in the open space. The Kennedy Art Center stood prominently on our left side. Its rainbow-colored lights glowed through the dark and reflected on the river, appearing to hover over the water.

On our right, a few headlights moved along the lanes of the arched Key Bridge that connected Georgetown to Rosslyn, Virginia, where skyscrapers towered over the riverbank unconstrained by DC's height restrictions for buildings.

"It's chilly out here." Elise crossed her arms across her chest for warmth and leaned against me. A petite gold chain dropped down the cleavage of her deep V-neck dress.

"Are you cold?" I said. "I should get you a cab home."

"Do you want to come over for another drink at my hotel?" She threw her hair behind her shoulder. "Saba, I don't want to be alone tonight . . ."

"What do you mean?"

She wrapped her arms around me and pressed her chest against my arm. "C'mon, you know what I mean!"

"Ha! I don't think your boyfriend would approve."

"I don't think he cares," she insisted.

I stared at her, surprised by her answer. "Are you serious?"

"How should I put this?" She searched for words. "Dan and I are in an open relationship. We're not exclusive."

"What?! For real? And you're cool with that?"

"I'm fine with it!"

"Still, the fact that you're my friend's girlfriend, or anybody's girlfriend, makes you off-limits to me."

"Oh, Saba, you're such a keeper," she said, disappointed. "Oh well, thanks for showing me around and taking me to the piano bar. That was fun!"

"Of course! I'm sure I will see you again when I get back to the other side of the Atlantic."

Jazz in Bangkok

o·o·o·o·o·o·o·o·o·o·o·o·o·o·o·o·o·o·o·

Bangkok is just like it is in the movies: girls are pretty, the food is spicy, and the traffic is terrible.

Lines of cars moved at a snail's pace. The only fast-moving things were scooters and fumes escaping from the exhaust pipes of stationary cars. Compelled to keep the engines running, commuters hopelessly waited for the traffic to clear.

I looked out the rear-seat window, trying to take in as much of the city's skyline as possible. An endless stream of flashing billboards and glaring headlights drifted by. It was about seven at night.

The gruesome experience of driving through downtown Bangkok was a perfect metaphor for how hard it would be for a small African company to break into the enormous market in Southeast Asia. As the new head of our nascent Asia operations, I had been tasked with establishing business partners in Bangkok. Since my trip to Canada, Mr. Sadiki had kept giving me travel assignments abroad.

I had been in Washington, DC, for months and might spend a few weeks in Thailand. Eventually, I purchased new clothes to update my outfit rotation as I moved from freezing weather to moderately cold to a tropical climate in Thailand. Mr. Sadiki had insisted I meet people in person rather than virtually. He was old-school like that. He believed in personal connections in business and in friendship. Given that we could only break into this market by working with established players, he wanted me to secure partnerships with local companies in the tourism industry.

"Where are you . . . ?" my cab driver mumbled.

I was listening but I wasn't hearing. My head was still jet-lagged from the long flight I had taken a few days earlier from Washington, DC, to Bangkok through Amsterdam. Each leg of the trip was at least seven hours long, and sleeping on planes or anything moving was a problem for me.

"What's that?"

"Where are you from?" he asked again with a heavy accent.

"Ah, I am from Rwanda." My eyes were looking out the window to admire Bangkok's skyline jungle.

"What?" he yelled above the traffic noise.

"I am from America!" I changed my answer.

"Ah, America! Good!" he said without taking his eyes off the road. "I know good bars. I can take you now!"

"Now?" I said with a weak smile. "I can't go now. You know I have plans!"

"Look here!" Undeterred, he waved a brochure over his shoulder, which I grabbed from his hand.

Moon Bar, Red Sky, floating market, golden Buddha, custom-made suits . . . I browsed through the ads on the colorful pamphlet, which had one phone number printed in bold letters at the bottom of the page.

"And you do all these?"

"Yes, sir! I can take you to buy excellent suits now."

"No, I am meeting someone," I said with a firmer voice this time. "Maybe another time. I will keep the brochure just in case."

The aggressive marketing strategy was as ingenious as it was annoying. Taxis stuck in traffic inevitably had the attention of their passengers; it was a golden opportunity for businesses to lure in new customers in a city of about ten million people and an equal number of business ventures. On second thought, I should have ridden one of the tuk-tuks, which seemed to zigzag around jammed roads without a problem.

When we finally arrived at my destination, I congratulated myself for avoiding an unexpected detour to my cab driver's tailoring shop.

Satisfaction dawned on me as I lifted myself out of my cab. So far away from home, I would never have imagined being here or my boss entrusting me with representing my company an ocean away. My driver probably didn't know where Rwanda was on a map or even that it was a country. Still, here I was—a kid born and raised in a small landlocked nation working on business deals in Asia's Jewel City. Bangkok was the El Dorado of the tourism industry. It had ranked as the most visited city globally for two consecutive years, ahead of London and Paris.

I was the most traveled person in my family at this point. Yet I had to dig deeper within myself to find the drive to aim for even more heights in my life, lest being the first to achieve things became a distraction. I feared that my relative accomplishments would inflict that sweet infirmity on me and make me complacent.

My mom would always tell me, "Saba, it's now or never! You should aim as high as you can." She had embodied this principle herself. She was the first person in her family to graduate from high school. However, life happened when she got her high school diploma. She got married and had to take care of her kids. It wasn't until much later, when my brother and I were in college, that she got the time and opportunity to fulfill her dream. She surprised everyone and enrolled in school to get that college degree she'd always wanted. She joked that she would beat my brother and me in completing coursework.

We tried to talk her out of her enrollment. She had already made history in our eyes, regardless of a college degree. But, she would say, making history is not the point; learning is!

I walked into a saxophone bar and scanned the red room.

The bar looked like an exotic record store. Picture frames and artifacts decorated the walls in a half-sacred, half-hipster manner, a mélange of Western and Oriental traditions characteristic of the city.

Jen waved at me as soon as I arrived and gestured for me to join her. She had secured us a table on the balcony overlooking the oval-shaped bar. The venue arranged the seating around the musicians, who stood behind stands that held their music sheets.

The audience sat tranquil, drinking local beer, as an indefatigable lead singer rocked his body to the dominant cry of the trombone.

"How long have you lived in Bangkok?" I asked Jen after I took a seat next to her.

"About five years now," she said.

"I bet you speak the local language now, huh? It took me three tries to get a cab driver to the right destination." I smiled.

Jen was Filipino. She had immigrated to Bangkok to operate an international travel and hospitality company in the city. I had set up the meeting to determine if Jen could be our point of contact in the city. Her experience and the process she had gone through to set up shop here were useful to my company.

"So, we're trying to build partnerships in Southeast Asia with someone who has experience working in this market," I said to initiate the discussion.

"Tell me again, how did you find our contact information?" Jen said.

An imposing dark-red velvet drape decorated one side of the room and muted the bright reds of framed portraits all around it. Everything was red at the bar, from floor carpets to chair cushions. Even the neon lights cast a crimson shadow against the walls.

"Chris," I said. "I got it from *Canadian Traveller* magazine. He's the one who suggested I reach out to you."

"Excuse me!" a woman who looked to be in her seventies yelled at us as she bumped my shoulder trying to reach her seat.

The crowd sat unimpressed by the musicians, except for this woman. However, the bar was almost at capacity. Virtually every chair in the bar had an occupant. Either showing up in silent admiration was people's way of expressing support, or maybe the drinks were tasty here!

When the band started playing "Sweet Caroline," Jen and I—who had finished off a few beers and were bubbling over in excitement as the conversation moved from professional to friendly—stood up and started dancing, waving our hands, and toasting everyone who looked our way at the bar.

The piercing gaze of the old woman beside me forced me to drop into my seat almost immediately. I wasn't privy to the country's cultural etiquette, so I tamed my enthusiasm lest I offend the locals.

"Hey, you! Where are you from?" the woman said as soon as I sat back down.

"America!" I said.

"America?" She shook her head. I thought of changing my answer to something else, but it was too late.

"How come she seems angry at me? What did I do?" I turned to Jen.

"She thinks we are together and that you are one of those sex tourists," Jen said without looking at me. She kept her sights on the musicians, slightly rocking her head to the beat.

"Well, she can rest easy. I'm just here for work. Goodness!"

The beer was influencing my judgment. I wondered why Jen had suggested we meet at a jazz bar, not an office or a coffee shop, which would be more appropriate for a business meeting.

"Saba, is this your first time in Bangkok?"

"Yes," I said. "By the way, Chris suggested I hit the red-light district while I'm here. I think he's crazy!"

"I can take you there," Jen said.

"That would be a hard pass for me. Don't give grandma here one more reason to hate me."

"Oh darling, that ship has sailed!" Jen smiled at me. "I think we should go. Wear a condom, and you'll be fine!"

I had been to the red-light district in Amsterdam. It didn't look that lewd from what I saw behind the glass. Girls sat behind windows knitting. Bangkok, however, was in a league of her own. I worried that if I ever saw what was happening in the district's strip, I might never unsee it.

"Someone else preoccupies my heart, Jen," I said to end the flirtatious talk.

Not too far from the libertine streets of Bangkok, Buddha monuments stood tall around the buoyant capital coated in gold. Monks vested in bright orange garments were a common sight in the city. They roamed the streets seeking good karma and enlightenment. Spiritual devotion and debauchery had somehow found a shared home in Bangkok.

"Where are you from?" the old woman asked again, swinging a beer bottle back and forth with her right hand.

The gaze of her red eyes burned with both disdain toward me and the copious amount of alcohol she had ingested. From that moment, my eyes were continually on her hand's movements. I feared she would decide to avenge the sins Western tourists committed in her home city and smash the bottle against my head in collective punishment.

Before long, Jen and I stood from our table and passed through the bar crowd, seated in an orderly manner, chatting, and listening to music. We headed toward a flickering Exit sign before hailing a cab back to my hotel, the Radisson Blu hotel in downtown Bangkok, and taking the elevator to the rooftop bar.

I was acutely aware that Jen was still with me. The alcohol had weakened my restraints and professional boundaries.

o · o · o · o · o · o ·

WE SAT OVERLOOKING THE CITY's skyline; the lights made the city's major arteries and high rises look like arrows into the sky. It was so nice to enjoy the view away from the roar of car engines and the throngs of pedestrians.

My conversation with Jen had now veered to the personal. Her cunning ability to blur the lines had won me over in the end. She was the only agent here who had agreed to meet with me on that day. A couple of other potential business partners had postponed their appointments. I was to stay here for a couple more weeks to reschedule them.

"So, who's this girl of yours?"

"I met her back home, but we're not together yet," I told Jen.

"Not together yet?" she said. "How come?"

"It's a long story, but the short version is that she asked me to wait two years before we can be together."

"What? You actually waited for her?"

"What do you know?" I smiled.

My decision was undoubtedly atypical, but I expected this reaction from people and was at peace with it. They say there's plenty of fish in the pond, but there was only one for me: Karen.

Some of my friends warned me I would regret wasting time with someone unwilling to commit. Others, mainly female, simply got mad at Karen, even if they had never met her. They would say she was keeping me hostage and robbing other girls of the opportunity to date me. Puzzled by my decision, or indecision, as they would call it, they talked about me and my love life as if I were a teenage boy seduced by a much older woman. As if I lacked any sort of agency or freedom to choose how to live my own life. The more they warned me against waiting for Karen, the more I wanted to do so, and my anticipation grew day by day . . .

My love life was as unconventional as my career had been. I'd left my office job to become a travel agent, and that decision had paid off. Hopefully, my commitment to Karen would end up as prosperous as my new career had been.

Karen wouldn't commit sooner, and I couldn't understand why. As time passed, however, the biggest worry in my life wasn't that my choices would fail, but that I would fail to make my own choices.

Before I'd quit my job, every decision about my career wasn't mine. I would solicit and choose the direction and perspectives of my trusted friends, family, and authority figures. I would model my life on what I perceived to be society's expectations. One evening, I'd turned the corner.

I'd been leaving work that night, exhausted and disillusioned by my life. It had hit me that erasing myself was inappropriate and counterproductive to myself and others. I'd decided then to quit my job and find my voice, to learn to discern it from the noise and confusion and heed its gentle cry.

When the server brought a couple of margaritas and handed them to Jen and me, my watch read 11:04 p.m. Jen wore her dark textured hair down, and it nearly entirely covered the blue denim jacket she was wearing.

"She doesn't deserve you, Saba," Jen said, holding her glass. She extended her legs and hooked her heels on the railing as she vented on my behalf. Her petite frame barely occupied half the wooden chair next to me. "If I were you, I would have moved on long ago!"

"The thought crossed my mind, trust me."

"When will you see this girl again?"

"Her name is Karen," I said. "I will see her when I leave Bangkok. The wait is almost over."

"I applaud your resolve, Saba. That's novel-worthy material, I tell you! You should write a book about it when you guys become a couple."

We sat silently next to each other as the gentle wind caressed our faces.

"Jen, do you think she will say yes when I ask her again?"

"Well, I'm rooting for you! You seem like a great guy." Her eyes connected with mine. "I mean, I'd say yes!"

"Thanks, Jen!" I smiled, though that last comment caught me off guard.

"I'll tell you what?" I said. "I promise I will write a book about our story if she says yes and send you an autographed copy."

A yellow glow hovered over the endless landscape of tall buildings as if it were a sacred city.

I was here in passing and would leave Jen behind with no assurances of ever seeing her again. I wasn't sure what Mr. Sadiki would decide about a partnership with her company. From what I had gathered, her company was as lean as ours. I was skeptical that it could manage international partners at this point, unless we hired someone to live and work with her team, which was what we were trying to avoid.

The constant travels had taken a toll on me. I had started to resent connecting with people, only to leave them behind as soon as the next destination called.

By this point, I had walked through the streets of Thailand, flown over Victoria Falls in Zambia, and scaled Mount Royal in Quebec. Still, as epic as those adventures were, I felt a pressing need to give up the constant stream of new experiences and new faces and settle down somewhere. I longed for a familiar face and a companion who would stay.

My world travels had made me realize that life is best when shared. It wasn't so much the places I visited that mattered anymore. Instead, it was the company that made the experience memorable. Being with a loved one in the middle of nowhere would make me happier than visiting the world's seven wonders alone. I wanted to share my life and have many more adventures with Karen. Waiting for her had heightened the anticipation of our upcoming reunion.

"Thanks for suggesting the jazz bar, Jen!" I said as we walked toward the elevator.

Inside, I pressed buttons for both thirty-seven, my floor, and the lobby. Low-key music played as the elevator rushed downward. I hugged Jen goodbye and quickly exited the elevator when we got to the thirty-seventh floor. I stepped out and looked back. Jen's deep brown eyes stared at me until the closing doors sealed in front of her face.

o · o · o · o · o · o ·

THE PHONE RANG AS SOON as I got to my room. I checked the caller's ID and swiped at the answer key on my phone screen.

"Dan! What's up?"

"Hi, Saba, where are you now?"

"I'm in Bangkok," I said. "What time is it in Kigali? It's almost midnight here."

"I thought you were here already. When do you get back? We need to talk."

"Yeah? I'll be back in about two weeks. I still have a few meetings before I leave. What's the matter?"

"Let's chat when you get back, okay?" Dan said. His voice was thick, as if he was anxious about something.

"Is everything all right?"

"Yeah, it's all right," Dan said. "Let's chat when you get back, since you'll be here soon."

"Are you sure about that?"

"Yeah, definitely. Safe travels back, man!"

"Okay, talk soon!" I hung up the phone.

His tone left me curious. What was so important that he couldn't tell me on the phone? Was it a family issue, a health issue, money, or relationships?

Dan didn't know enough about where I stood on the first three to have an opinion. I had hung out with him and Elise a few times, but he had never met my relatives. He knew little about my job and health. Only Karen had met my mother, as I had brought her to my mom's house for lunch on Sunday on a couple of occasions.

Dan knew about Karen, however. In fact, he had been in touch with her, according to Elise. She told me that Dan frequently contacted Karen about business. But a part of me didn't buy that.

The business consulting firm Dan worked for only operated in Rwanda, as far as I knew. Businesses certainly expanded across borders, but of all the fifty-plus countries in Africa, what were the chances that his company would pick Zambia as its next market destination? There had to be another convenient reason behind their communication.

I couldn't fathom why Dan would hit on Karen in the first place or why Karen would go along with it. Dan didn't strike me as her type, but what did I know? Despite being in a relationship, Dan and Elise had erased sexual boundaries. They were in an open relationship, so there was that!

I opened the small fridge door in my room, poured a glass of wine, and chugged it as I struggled to put all the pieces together.

If Dan and Karen were cheating behind my back, Elise would have to know about it. Or worse, she would have to be in on it.

Karen didn't mention or hint at anything along those lines when we talked, however. She had called the day after I got to Bangkok to tell me she was back in Kigali and wanted us to go see Ismaël Lô perform. Unfortunately, my return flight would land the day after the festival.

We had talked about how things had come full circle. Two years earlier, we had learned Ismaël Lô was coming to town on our first date. We reminisced about that day, about all the things we had in common, including how much we loved live music. Her voice sounded teary when I told her I wouldn't be back in time to go to the KigaliUp festival with her, but we made plans to see each other as soon as I got back.

As for Elise, she'd said nothing to me when she visited Washington, DC. Instead, she'd made a move on me. Maybe it was because she was feeling guilty or compensating for something. What struck me more wasn't the moment of attempted impropriety. Rather, she'd admitted her boyfriend wouldn't care if we hooked up that night. Was all this part of some devious plan to have everyone sleep with everyone?

Soon enough, I would find out if waiting for Karen had been worth the trouble. Or perhaps I would discover, in a troubling twist of events, that my closest friends had betrayed me in pursuit of a four-way love affair!

I reached into my pocket and pulled out a wrapped golden elephant necklace I had bought for Karen in Bangkok. I looked at it for a while before sliding it into my backpack pocket next to my passport.

It wasn't because I was in Thailand that I picked an elephant necklace. Instead, it was because of what the majestic animal represents. Elephants have an excellent memory and remember good things that happen to them. They are loyal.

I pulled down my bedding and climbed inside the sheets. My head rested against the soft pillow, facing the window of my hotel room. Bangkok's skyline glowed in front of me like a constellation of stars. Specks of lights from buildings below lit up the city, fighting away the darkening night.

I wrapped the bedding around my body, shivering from air-conditioning and anxiety. I closed my eyes and faded into slumber, hoping that the next day would bring answers to my love life.

KigaliUp

o·o·o·o·o·o·o·o·o·o·o·o·o·o·o·o·o·o·o·o·

Afitter a cold shower, I sat on my very own bed, lacing my
leather shoes. When I got home, I found out someone had
broken our external water heater, but no one was in the
house that night. Any noise I made in the room sounded louder
than usual, almost eerie. I had been away for too long, and the place
was simply too spacious for one person and a live-in houseboy. The
house had a four-car parking garage, a yard, and a small bungalow
with a barbecue grill—not that we ever used the grill, but it was an
excellent decor for the yard. My former roommate Kamana had
moved out when he got married. I had stayed in the same house and
covered his share of the five-hundred-dollar-a-month rent while I
looked for another place—or a new roommate . . .

My suitcase lay open on the floor, and an explosion of clothes
and shoes mingled together in every direction. A painting of the
Potomac River stuck out from its paper bag beside other souvenirs.

I had bought it at Galerie L'Enfant, an antique shop in Washington, DC.

After successfully changing my return flight from Bangkok, I'd arrived in Kigali sooner than I had initially planned. Karen was at the music festival but didn't expect me to arrive until the following day. I wanted to surprise her.

I paced between my room and the adjacent bathroom, forgetting what I was looking for. I went back to the bathroom. When I looked in the mirror, I realized I had a three-day beard. I walked back to my room and checked my suitcase for my comb and electric razor.

I closed my eyes at the buzzing noise of the razor, almost falling asleep to its rattling sound. I had waited for this moment for a long time. Somehow, time had gone by way too quickly since the day I had asked Karen out.

A lot had changed since then, but deep down, I was the same kid who'd dreamed of traveling to different countries and changing the world. I wasn't sure exactly how I would do that, but I thought my life was a journey to find out how, or if nothing else, to find myself! That feeling hadn't changed over the years—well, that and my love for Karen. I loved her as much as I had when I'd first asked her to be with me.

What will Karen say this time? How will she react when she sees me at the concert? And what will happen if she finally says yes? Questions ran through my head as I sat on my bed, waiting for my cab to arrive. Sweat broke out under my arms, drawing dark circles on my shirt, as I thought through options.

It was about 9:30, and the KigaliUp festival was in its last hours. I hoped to catch the last couple of artists, as they featured headliners last. "Let's do this!" I said, standing in front of the mirror one final time.

A loud honk burst outside my house, and my heart almost jumped out of my rib cage. The taximan I'd called had arrived and was impatiently waiting outside.

I tucked my shirt into my dark blue pants in a hurry, slipped the elephant necklace I had bought in Bangkok into my pocket, and slammed the door shut behind me.

We reached the traffic circle near the Gisimenti building and headed toward Amahoro Stadium, the biggest stadium in Kigali, whose name means "peace" in the local language. People and cars were everywhere; the festival added more traffic to an already congested road juncture.

The time on my phone was 10:07 p.m., and Ismaël Lô, the famous Senegalese singer, was headlining the festival again two years after his debut performance. He was performing at 10:00 p.m. Unable to make my cab go faster, I leaned back on my seat cushion and closed my eyes. The chorus of car engines and outside noises suddenly intensified.

A gust of wind mixed with exhaust fumes leaking from cars and swerving taxi motos blasted into my squinting face. The car window was open, as the old Toyota Corolla was without air-conditioning.

After several hours of flight time, my head buzzed from the outside noise. I prayed that the three cups of coffee I had consumed would keep me up a little longer to talk to Karen and watch the last performance. My phone lit up on my lap, and I navigated toward the note app and opened the short poem I had penned for Karen several months prior.

Whenever I missed Karen or thought of her, I'd open my phone and update the years, months, weeks, or days in the last verse, counting down to the day she would be mine. So, I changed the last line and replaced the phrase "in two days" with "today."

I thought I should forget as you fly away
for living apart surely meant no pathway
easy come, easy go, they say
I will find another girl I like the same way
but memories of Tanganyika and that divey bar
keep flashing back as I love you from afar
I will see you in a city so familiar
today I marked my calendar

o · o · o · o · o · o ·

"CAN I GET A TICKET, please?" I said to an ambulatory ticket seller.

"Well, the show's almost over." He looked at me, stunned.

There were no lines at the stadium entrance, as most people were already inside.

"It's all good, my friend," I said. "I would have paid the same if only Ismaël Lô was playing."

The event organizers had redecorated the stadium's outside area. A poster image of Ismaël Lô dressed in a white boubou stretching from his shoulders to below his knees hung prominently at the gate. Dazzling lights shone brightly from atop the main stage, next to which was a massive screen projection. The lights turned the crowd in front of the stage into moving shadows.

I didn't text Karen. Instead, I tried using my sixth sense to detect her in the crowd. It would be a perfect surprise.

I zigzagged toward the front of the crowd, stumbling by people and beer bottles littered on the ground. I kept moving forward until I couldn't find space to squeeze through anymore. As I neared the safety railing that they had fixed between the musicians and the standing audience, the crowd got thicker and thicker.

Ismaël Lô played his guitar with closed eyes and sang with a kepi hat on his head. His signature instrument, the harmonica, hung around his neck, close to his lips, waiting for the most climactic moment of the performance to play its part.

Flashing lights beamed from the platform at the rhythm of the beat. Gently rocking their heads, backup singers sang along at their turn. All of them were dressed in blue boubous. You could tell the crew had performed together for a long time and had passed worrying about whether they played the right chords. They knew they would. With ease, they produced the music, seemingly feeling the soul of the songs and ruminating on the memories they evoked.

The next song only needed a few strokes of guitar strings to make the crowd insane. This was the time for the most iconic piece, "Tajabone."

Switching to a one-man performance, Ismaël Lô sent his crew offstage for a break. He would play the guitar and the harmonica and sing alone. Screams flew from all over the concert venue. Ismaël Lô played the song's intro, and the audience started singing before his lips touched the microphone. They beat him to his own song, and he let them. He kept quiet and let us sing the first few verses as he played the guitar.

A smile grew on his face; he knew how to connect with his crowd. His song, the fruit of his creative mind, had become the song of his audience. It encapsulated the universe of stories each individual associated with it. Ismaël Lô's face beamed with satisfaction. His music transcended the mere harmony of voice and instruments to embody people's experiences. The sound of each instrument stroked both the ears and the heart at the same time.

A woman in her twenties next to me had her eyes fixated on her favorite artist. She sang at the top of her lungs, mixing the song's lyrics with raw screams of excitement. The intensity of her shouts spoke of something profound, of memories of life endured and buried, which the song unearthed. The notes drew out memories of people, of places, of adventures.

The melody of "Tajabone" transported me back to my childhood, to the Ngagara neighborhood where our house was located: the humidity of the plains of Bujumbura, kids playing soccer in dusty alleys with bare feet, the songs of itinerant peanut vendors walking the neighborhood streets. And it was in that city that I fell in love.

Karen had walked the same streets of my neighborhood. She had seen my elementary school and the benches I'd sat on as a kid. That part of me was also a part of her story now. I wanted to add to our story line the ultimate ending: Karen and me together as a couple.

This was the moment. I wanted to find Karen and tell her how much I loved her. Remind her of the good times. Tell her she was worth the wait.

My eyes bounced left and right, trying to find her figure in the crowd. I craned my neck and retreated from the stage, trying to catch sight of her. I moved further away from the crowd and headed toward the back, to stairs leading inside the stadium. The organizers had built the show set right outside the stadium.

My ears still buzzing from loud music, I walked toward the food trucks vendors had set up to feed people. The smell of cigarettes, beer, and grilling burgers hit my face. My head twisted and looked in different directions, sifting through unfamiliar faces. A few people sat down the stairs, away from the crowd, eating, drinking, and snuggling.

When I was about to give up and reach for my phone, I saw, just a stone's throw away from me, in a small penumbra, a woman wearing her hair in a ponytail. She was kissing a man, leaning against one of the stadium's staircase walls.

"Wait, I know that girl . . . ," I said to a vendor, as if he cared. "No way!" I screamed. "Karen!"

Uninterrupted, the couple kept going at it, shifting angles and kissing. Their lust and the loud music insulated them from everything else around them.

"Oh my gosh! You gotta be kidding me! I know that guy too! No, freakin' way! It's freakin' AB! Karen's hooking up with freakin' Albert! That is so messed up!"

"Is there a problem, sir?" the vendor asked, annoyed by my rant. I turned toward the vendor without uttering another word and stared at him.

"Saba! Saba!" a woman's voice called behind me.

I rotated again and saw Elise and Dan standing near a small line of people at the next vendor's truck.

"Look who's here," Dan said, smiling and walking toward me. He stopped when he saw my face was blank. "Hey, are you okay?"

I did not hug them. I still couldn't say a word, even though I hadn't seen them in months.

"How could you guys do this to me?" I broke.

"Do what, Saba?" Elise shouted, raising her voice above the noise.

My eyeballs stared at them in shock. I turned and looked toward Karen and Albert again. They were still making out.

Elise and Dan followed my gaze and saw them too.

Albert's left hand pressed against Karen's lower back; his other hand intertwined with hers. She tilted her head upward to meet his ugly lips hanging above her face.

"My God, I can't watch this!" I sighed.

"Dude, I wanted to tell you! That's why I called you." Dan said.

"This is what you called me for?" I gestured with my hand. "You knew?"

"Sorry, man! I wish I had told you sooner after Karen told me." Dan said.

"Karen told you?!" I hollered. "This is so messed up!"

"They've been dating for a while, but Karen was worried about how you might react," he said.

"How long have you known this?" I said. "How could you not give me a heads-up? You know I'm crazy about her."

"I am so sorry, Saba!" Elise said.

"So, you also knew about it when you came to DC and didn't tell me?"

"I didn't know then. Dan told me shortly after I left."

"Still," I said, "you could have told me if you wanted to. This is ridiculous!"

My knees were shaking as if they couldn't hold my weight anymore. I hit the ground like a felled tree. I sat in the dirt, almost in a fetal position, my head buried in the palms of my hands.

"Saba, are you okay?" Elise said.

"Hey, take your time," Dan said. "We'll stay here with you." He squatted and placed his hand on my shoulder.

"No, you guys should leave," I said. "Just leave me alone!"

"Can we give you a ride home?" Dan said.

"I'd like to be alone, please. Don't worry about me," I said. "I'll take a cab home."

My stomach twisted with exhaustion and angst. I collected myself from the ground, silently dusted off my pants, and headed toward the stadium exit without looking back.

As I walked away, I wanted to check if Karen and her new boyfriend were still in the same position. I tried to look at the face of betrayal one more time, but I couldn't. The sight was too painful!

The Art Café

Karen sat at the table in the café's garden. She had beaten me to our appointment. I hadn't given her the courtesy of sending a text saying I was running late. I mean, what was the point? It was like showing up late to a funeral.

Against my wishes never to speak to Karen again, Dan and Elise had arranged for Karen and me to meet a couple of days after the music festival. They insisted I needed to talk to her, and they made sure she knew I had seen her with Albert at the concert.

The mood was otherwise upbeat at the trendy café. Seated two by two, customers smiled and checked things on each other's phone screens. A giant clock hung next to the counter, its ticking hand reminding everyone that time was running out. Bags of coffee beans branded with the company's logo lined the shelves underneath the clock. Their earthy aroma pervaded the coffee shop, only interrupted by the cigarette smoke from a nearby table.

The manager of the café, a young man in his midtwenties, was roasting coffee beans outside, inviting the inquisitive looks of customers curious to watch and learn about the coffee roasting process.

I headed toward the backyard, where Karen waited underneath the shade of a parasol planted in the grass. The café was near a major road intersection. Cars and motorcycles roared behind us as motorists stopped and started their engines at traffic lights.

"Hey!" I nodded to Karen and sat on the wooden bench beside her.

"Have you been to this place before?" she said.

"I haven't. This must be a new coffee shop," I said, reluctant to engage in small talk.

Low-key jazz music played in the background out of a hidden speaker.

"This one is unfamiliar. When we would go out, I used to be the one to pick restaurants, remember?" I offered reluctantly.

"And I would pick the meals we would eat," she said with a shy smile.

Karen wore a black blouse and beige pants that day. Her hair was down and curly and looked as if it was still drying from a bath.

"How things have changed," I said. "I miss that time."

"Me too," Karen said without making eye contact.

We sat on an L-shaped bench at the coffee shop, looking straight ahead to avoid eye contact like two teenagers on a first date.

"That's what I don't understand, Karen. We seemed to have great chemistry. Where did we go wrong?"

Karen paused, her gaze fixed in front of her. I could see the sparkle in her left eye; tears welled as she thought about what to say.

Car engines rumbled as traffic lights turned green on the nearby road, disrupting the sense of intimacy the garden plants around us were trying hard to provide.

"I don't know," she said in a heavy voice. "Dan and Elise told me you were mad when you saw me with Albert." She looked at me. "But you and I aren't together, you know!"

With a scratchy throat, I struggled to utter my words. My limbs were weak, and my stomach hunched like a bow. I could feel the weight of my body against the wooden backrest as I leaned harder to find support.

"You know why we're not together, don't you, Karen? You didn't give us a chance! You asked me to wait for two freakin' years while you were screwing around with . . . Albert, of all people!"

"Did you actually wait for me?" Karen wiped tears off her face.

"Man, I hate that guy. He's like a mercenary. He only cares about himself!"

"Did you actually wait?" Karen said again.

"I changed my flight to come earlier to surprise you, Karen. I wanted to ask you again at the festival while Ismaël Lô played. It would have been the perfect moment. And now this."

Karen wiped tears off her blushing cheeks again.

"I'm so sorry, Saba! I honestly didn't believe you'd wait for me," she stuttered. "You travel a lot, and I'm sure you meet multiple women."

"Well, I waited for you, Karen! For two years, I've dated no one," I said. "I hoped you would do the same. That's all I was hoping for—that you'd wait for me too! Am I crazy for asking that? You're the one who asked me to wait for two years in the first place, for goodness' sake!"

"I am sorry, Saba! You didn't even hook up with anyone?"

I gazed at the sky before burying my head in my hands.

"See! That's what I thought," she snapped before I could respond.

"Okay, I have a confession to make," I sighed. "Something happened in Montreal with this woman I met after you left." I bit my lip as I explained. "But it's not the same, I promise."

"It doesn't matter! You had sex with another woman. So why do you get pissed when I do the same?"

"You had sex with Albert? Please stop! I can't . . ."

My head sank into my hands again. I wished this entire conversation was a bad dream, that someone would pinch me and wake me up.

"Look! I waited for you," I tried to start over.

"Doesn't look like it to me!"

I realized I had lost any moral high ground to assign blame.

"Look, I failed once during a low moment. I never told you, but I had a cancer scare after you left."

"What!?" she said. "Are you just making excuses now?"

Because I had concealed the news from Karen until this contentious moment, it made it harder for her to believe me. I wanted to forget everything that had happened in Montreal that night, and the fewer the people who knew about it, the quicker I had hoped to leave it all behind.

"Look, can we not be mad at each other for a second?" I said. "This isn't the reunion I had wished for."

"I can't believe you're having a holier-than-thou attitude when you've done exactly the same thing." She shook her head.

"Karen, it's not like that! I'm not dating that girl. I like you, okay? I'm crazy about you, and seeing you with another man hurts. Do you understand that?"

Indeed, I had waited for Karen until a weak moment had caught me off guard in Montreal. That moment of, should I say, indiscretion was about to void all the efforts I had made over the past two years.

I regretted booking a private room for comfort that night in Montreal. In hindsight, I should have slept in a shared dorm room on a bunk bed. When I'd mentioned my private room to Moira at the tiki bar that night, she'd suggested we return to the hostel and sneak in a bottle of wine. It was against hostel policy to bring in alcohol from outside, but we did it anyway, more to feel the high of breaking the rules than because we wanted wine. We didn't even drink the bottle. Moira didn't let us.

She sat me on the bed as soon as we got to my room. Her delicate hands touched me, pressed against my chest, and walked me backward until my legs hit the bed frame. Until she trapped me. I had nowhere to go.

She pulled her miniskirt up her slender thighs and sat on my lap. From that point on, she unleashed the floodgates. Her eyes were piercing. She had turned into a different person, fierce, raw, primal.

She ripped her crop top off and flashed her crimson velvet underwear. The shadow of her face covered me as she leaned over me. Her parted lips looked silky yet violent, like a whirlpool sucking me into a place I'd never been before, rushing me into deep waters.

I fumbled for the clasps on her bra and snapped it open. I could taste the liquor on her lips and tongue as she kissed me. She whispered in my ear, things I can't remember to this day. All I recall is that I felt safe in her arms. Her hair draped over my face like a shroud, sheltering me from anxiety, the precarity of life, and the perils of our existence.

My body burned with passion as her hands ran along my tingling skin. Her scent stayed on me for three days after that night. I couldn't tell whether it was her natural odor or the perfume she had worn that rubbed off on my clothes.

Until then, my life had been all about playing by the rules: written rules, unwritten rules, arbitrary rules like waiting for Karen for two years. That night, however, I changed.

I begged Moira to stay with me, given it was late, but she refused.

"You don't live here," she had objected with sadness in her eyes. After we were done, she kissed my lips hard one last time, picked up her leather boots and other things from the floor, and stumbled out of my room. She left me an unopened bottle of pinot gris and a bittersweet memory, one I knew would come to haunt me one day.

"Karen," I said, "is there a way we can put this behind us and try again?"

"You won't like my answer!" she said. Despite her uncontrollable crying, Karen sounded decisive, as if she knew I would ask that. As if she had rehearsed her answers beforehand.

"Karen, do you like me anymore?"

She looked at me, her blushing cheeks covered in tears.

"I'm with Albert now," she said.

"I get it," I said. "Well, I don't, but I have nothing else to say."

"Look, Saba," she said, "you're such a great guy, and—"

"Please, stop!"

"You get me really well. I'd like us to stay friends," she said. "I don't want to lose you."

"Hey, there you are!" Dan and Elise announced themselves from a distance when they saw us.

Karen wiped tears off her face.

"We don't mean to interrupt. We were just checking on you," Elise said.

"Actually, I think we're done here." My eyes avoided contact with Karen's.

"Can we give you guys a ride home if you're headed out? I insist!" Dan said, sensing our hesitation.

Dan's car was outside the café entrance. I took the passenger seat next to Dan while Karen sat in the back next to Elise.

I rolled my window down so the wind would blow my eyes dry, but it had the opposite effect. Tears poured down my cheeks in silence as Dan's RAV4 sped down Kigali's green hills. I put my shades on, lifting them up from time to time to wipe tears off my face with a napkin I had collected at the coffee shop. Karen was blowing her running nose, and Elise comforted her.

"Are you guys going to be okay?" Elise said.

"Thanks, Elise!" I said. "Can we please change the subject?"

Unlike our first ride together, when I'd taken the group hiking the Virunga Mountains, it wasn't rainy and muddy outside. Instead, we were cruising through the smooth paved roads of Kigali on a bright cloudless day.

The gloom and showers weren't from the skies above this time; they were from our sore eyes and broken hearts.

The necklace I'd bought for Karen in Bangkok was in my pocket. I reached for it and looked at the medal as it shone in the sun's light one last time, before burying it in my fist again. As the car sped on, I extended my arm out the window. I felt the sun's warmth on my skin, then the wind's forces against me, the pressure of gusts on my outstretched arm. I let go of my grip one finger at a time until the necklace fell from my hand.

"Did you throw something out the window?" Dan said.

"It's nothing."

I turned and looked at Karen one more time. Karen—the woman who had stolen my heart. The one I'd saved myself for, for two years . . . well, almost!

Last Note

○·

I am sitting at Inzora Café overlooking Kigali's skyline, writing the final chapter of this book. I can see the two tallest mountains in the city through the window wall—Mount Kigali and Mount Jali crossing each other like two lovers holding hands. The dry season is at its peak, and I can smell the hot air trapped inside the building as sunlight permeates the beige-tinted glass, lighting up the half bookstore, half coffee shop.

My Dakine backpack is next to my chair, its reflection gleaming in the smooth floor tiling beneath it. I reach out to the Type C plug hidden beneath the table and connect it to the power supply cable before adjusting the lighting on my computer screen to the maximum.

The girl at the coffee shop didn't ask me what I would have. She brought the usual as soon as she saw me walking in earlier. A glass of water, a medium-roast coffee, and a smoothie made of fresh mango, strawberries, and pineapple.

I have been coming here to write this book for a few weeks now, ever since I resigned from my job as a travel agent with MBT.

After a while, I couldn't bear working with Albert or the awkward hallway encounters with Karen when she would come to see him at the office. She had been making regular trips back from Zambia to see Albert.

Mr. Sadiki was furious when I left. He offered me a raise and tried to talk me into changing my mind. But I told him it was for personal reasons that I needed to step away for a while.

Realizing I was determined to move on, he assured me I would always have a place at his company if I ever wanted to return. Despite his mean-boss demeanor, he was loyal to his staff, a side of him I was pleased to discover in the end. I told him I was grateful for everything, especially for him taking a chance on me when I had no experience in the trade. MBT allowed me to realize my childhood dream to travel the world and, for what it's worth, to meet Karen. Without this opportunity and the people I met through MBT, I wouldn't have written this book, either.

I first got the idea of writing a book from Jen in Bangkok. "If you and this girl you've been waiting for eventually get together, write a book about it," she had urged me. This isn't the ending she assumed or hoped for, but I wrote the book anyway.

I wanted to write about the adventures of traveling to a distant land and the experience of trying to fit in, broadening one's horizons, career options, and worldview. I wanted to capture the travel bug that causes us to always wonder and jump on the next plane, train, or road trip to . . . well, anywhere! The memories that gave me thrills and the songs that made me relive them were what I wanted to write about.

I also wanted to immortalize the stories of people I met along the way: Guido, Naaj, Babu, Mutoka, Izzy, Abby, Father Dion and, yes, Moira! This book is about understanding and empathizing with one another and realizing that deep down, we are not that different. Sadness, happiness, fear, and hope are to be found everywhere.

This book is about the spiritual, the humane, and the mundane. It is about falling in love. But in the end, this book is not about Karen and Saba. It's about Saba.